BECOMING C

By Lisa Rose Fa

Becoming Cheryl by Lisa Rose Farrow is published by Lisa Rose Farrow Productions.

Copyright © March 2022

All rights are reserved. No portion of this book may be reproduced in any form whatsoever without expressed written permission of the publisher except as permitted by United States Copyright Law.

First edition March 2022

Becoming Cheryl

Contents

Dedication

We all have our fantasies. Sexual fantasies are the very best.
This book is lovingly dedicated to readers with sexual
fantasies of all types. May your fantasies come true for you,
even if only in your dreams.

Also, for Robin, who inspired this book with fantasies of her
own.

Preface

It is a compliment to all of us who are the object of desire, even if those boys who admire us are too shy to act. Sometimes all they need is a bit of encouragement to overcome their shyness.

Of course there are always those admirers that we don't really want in our life. We need to deal with them too.

Most of us will never know how many guys really adore us. Still, it is good for our ego to know that we are adored.

Prologue. Becoming Cheryl

Most girls find it amusing to see a boy dressed up like a girl.
They look cute that way, shy, timid, blushing embarrassingly
red. It would be fun to dress a boy up, but even more fun to
come upon a boy who has dressed himself up.

There are many reasons for a male to crossdress. But
crossdressing for love is by far the most passionate reason.

Such a boy would be so sexually turned on by the adventure
that he would hardly be able to control himself. He would be
putty in the hands of any girl who knew the truth about him.

Daryl Meeks will soon find out what that means.

Chapter 1. Daryl Meeks

Daryl Meeks had been longing for Robin Dearing for years. He first saw her back in high school, but he had never even approached her. Boys like Daryl are far too shy to approach a pretty girl like Robin.

Robin was everything that Daryl could ever want in a girl. She was intelligent, she was energetic, she had a beautiful smile, she had long beautiful hair, and she had the looks of a super model. In his eyes, Robin was an angel sent from heaven.

Most would say that Robin was out of Daryl's league. The fact that she ignored him proved it. But Daryl held out hope that someday, somehow, he would find a way to get to know her.

Ever since he could remember, Daryl had been the shy reserved type. Most certainly it was because of his looks. His small frame, fine features, girlish voice, and a general lack of hair, other than his full head of hair, meant that he was constantly being mistaken for a girl. He liked his hair long, so he wore it that way. That certainly didn't help.

Whenever he started a new school year, the new teacher would always start out by referring to him as a girl. They would look at him and say things like, "Daryl? That's an odd name for a girl." During the school year, girl pronouns would occasionally slip out and his classmates would laugh at his red-faced embarrassment.

As a result the boys ignored him. He had never had a real male friend. Since he wasn't very boyish, the girls ignored him too. The lone exceptions were Yvonne and Heather.

Daryl always felt like a pity friend with the two girls, but they were the only two who ever talked with him. They were social outcasts too. They were girls who spent Friday nights shopping instead of dating because they couldn't get dates. They asked Daryl along because they felt sorry for him. Daryl had spent many weekends with the girls while they perused the clothing aisles in stores that catered only to girls. It was humiliating for Daryl, but it was far better than staying home.

After high school graduation, Yvonne and Heather went their separate ways to college. That left Daryl without any friends. He just had an emptiness in his heart for Robin, the girl who he loved so much.

But now he was off to college too. His Stepmother had arranged everything in order to send him on his way. She had prepaid his apartment for a few weeks, paid for one semester of college complete with food card, and given him a small stipend of cash for incidentals. It was more than enough to tide him over until he could find work.

Apparently, Daryl had been the only thing between his new step mom and marital bliss. She had made it fairly clear that Daryl was grown up and it was time for him to leave the nest. So she had made it exceptionally easy for him to do so. Daryl had no plans to return home after graduation. He would graduate, get a job, and then support himself. There would be no need to go back home.

He had selected both his college and his major very scientifically. He simply followed Robin to the same college where she went. She had no idea that he had followed her, but follow her he did. They both stayed in the same apartment complex on campus, because all of the dormitories had been filled up. They were both going to study computer science—a topic that Daryl knew absolutely nothing about. But if it was okay with Robin to study computer science, then it was okay with him.

When orientation day came, Robin still hadn't noticed Daryl. Worse still, Daryl saw her talking with a guy who could have been a star athlete. Daryl knew that he had to do something quick, or he would lose Robin for good.

Now Daryl was back in his tiny one- bedroom apartment. He sat at the small work desk staring at his newly issued student identification card. Another mistake had been made that would need to be corrected. It was only then that the idea struck Daryl.

Maybe he had finally found a way to get closer to Robin.

Chapter 2. Cheryl Meeks

It was clearly a clerical error. Instead of Daryl Meeks, male, the student identification card said Cheryl Meeks, female. These things always seemed to happen to Daryl. He had been mistaken for a girl so many times that he didn't really think much of it. Nobody had even said anything about it when Daryl had attended the orientation session. When they checked him in, they obviously had thought that he was Cheryl Meeks, a female student.

The inspiration came when remembering how Robin looked after she talked with Mr. Athlete. She had sat alone by herself while the other students had milled around totally oblivious to her. Obviously, Robin didn't know anybody at her new school. What she needed was a friend.

Cheryl Meeks could be that friend!

Daryl looked at himself in the mirror that was on the wall just above his work desk. It was no wonder that they thought he was a girl. Even to himself, he had to admit that he was girlish. A new outfit here, a new hairdo there, and maybe a touch of makeup and nobody would be the wiser.

He had shopped before with Yvonne and Heather so he was familiar with women's clothing. There was also that time with his Mother before her divorce. More about that later.

Heck, these days he could go out online and get next day delivery of just about anything that he wanted. Classes weren't scheduled to start for for a few days so he had plenty of time to work things out.

4

He opened up his laptop computer and perused a few sites. It wouldn't even take too much money to pull it off. He had a wallet with cash in it, but there was no reason to use it. He put it down next to his laptop computer. Instead he took advantage of the University. The University had made things easy — they issued credit cards to every new student, curtesy of the local bank. His new credit card was issued to Cheryl Meeks. So why not use it? A click here and a click there and Cheryl Meeks was that much closer to reality.

Daryl imagined what kind of girl Cheryl Meeks would be. He selected daring clothes that only a popular girl might wear. He bought enough lingerie for every day of the week. Shoes! Girls like shoes, right? So he had to have more than one pair. So several pairs of shoes and a few other necessary accessories were added to the haul.

There was one big problem. Better make that one small problem. Daryl had heard about tucking and how it could help to make a boy appear to be a girl by hiding things down there. But he didn't know exactly how to do it. Not that his little penis was that noticeable. Everybody always seemed to think that he was a girl even though he had never been tucked.

After a quick Internet search, Daryl didn't think it would be a problem. He added a tight panty girdle to his order to keep things in place.

Chapter 3. Packages

There are many reasons for a guy to dress up like a girl. There are stage performances, costume parties, and even for sexual adventure. But for Daryl, his motivation was entirely different than any of those things. For Daryl, dressing up like a girl was for love. He felt like it was his best chance to get close to Robin.

Packages began to arrive the following morning. Daryl excitedly opened them and carefully laid the contents out on his bed. When the last of the packages had been opened, Daryl looked at the assortment of feminine clothing.

He was a bit overcome by it all. It had all seemed so simple when he ordered things one at a time, but now it seemed so different. An assortment of panties, panty girdles, bras, and pantyhose all looked intimidating. The two breast form boxes reminded him of his decision to look as feminine as possible.

Cheryl's outerwear appeared to be so sexy. Maybe *too* sexy. Miniskirts, tank tops, and short dresses didn't look quite so skimpy on line. The thought of wearing them in public was frightening.

There were cosmetics too. He had watched several on-line videos in order to purchase the right things. He would need to watch them again in order to do things properly. He would worry about that later.

Several pairs of heels told the story the best. The strappy sandals and the pumps all had high heels. Even if he managed to pull everything else together, he would be challenged to walk in them. Girls wore heels, guys don't.

Without them there might be questions. With them, no questions would be asked.

He had spent considerable time deciding how he should appear. He had mentally used Yvonne and Heather as models. Models of what *not* to do! Yvonne and Heather had always worn dowdy outfits. He reasoned that was why they were so unpopular. So he had selected short skirts, sheer blouses, tight sweaters, and a couple of flirty dresses for his alter ego. Cheryl wasn't going to be frumpy. She was going to be fashionable, and above all, popular.

In his excitement he had even purchased feminine nightgowns. If he was going to do it, he was going to go all out.

But looking at the flirty attire now, Daryl wasn't so sure if he had done the right thing. The outfits were very daring, perhaps too daring. But that was all he had to work with now. Provocative clothing would just have to do.

It was decision time. His future was spread out on the bed for him just waiting for an answer. He could almost hear *Cheryl* being whispered in his ear, seductively beckoning him to continue. Could he really become Cheryl Meeks just by putting on new clothes? Why not?

He knew that once he started down the Cheryl Meeks road that there could be no turning back. How could he ever explain to anybody why he dressed up like a girl? Nobody would ever understand.

He loved Robin. He had to face reality. A pretty girl like Robin would never even look at a guy like Daryl. He wasn't an athlete, he wasn't muscular, he wasn't an impressive specimen of masculinity. He certainly wasn't rich. No, he was just wimpy Daryl, a guy no girl would ever be interested in. Or so he thought.

He could see no way to get close to her other than to become her girlfriend. It was a novel idea. A brazen solution to a perplexing problem. A problem that he could not solve any other way. He knew that he could pull it off if he really wanted to.

He took a deep breath. Perhaps had he not have been so smitten with Robin he would have decided differently. But she had cast her spell and Daryl was fully taken in by her enticing charms. He could not resist himself any longer.

He gathered up all of his male clothing and placed it all into the same boxes that the feminine clothing had arrived in. He hadn't brought much with him, so there was considerable room to spare.

So, after taking another deep breath, he began to slowly peel off his clothes and put them in the boxes with the rest. He taped them all closed, sealing Daryl in for good. Then he moved them to the front door so that they would be easy to remove from the apartment. Later, after dark, he planned to dispose of it all in the dumpster that was behind the apartment complex.

 Finally, he stood naked next to the bed. Then he took a long look at himself in the full-length mirror that was on the back of the bedroom door. He was glad that he had thought to shave everywhere in the shower the night before. It's not that he had that much hair to remove, but now his legs looked feminine. He raised his arms. He looked feminine under his arms too. Finally he looked down to his clean-shaven genitals. Not a strand of hair there either!

He liked what he saw. Daryl was certain that he could pass. There was no doubt about it. He took one more deep breath.

Then Cheryl began to get dressed.

Chapter 4. Transformation

The first thing that Cheryl did was to reach for a bra. She needed one for every day of the week, so she had bought several of them, in various full figure styles. This time she selected a strapless bra—she wanted to go daring on her first day. She struggled a bit trying to clip her first bra on before she decided to clip it on in front and then rotate it into position. After she had it in place, she felt silly with the large deflated cups.

No problem there. She immediately reached for her breast forms. Once she slid the first one into position, she was immediately glad that she had selected size D. Her thought was that small breasts might be a giveaway, but size D cups filled out would help sell her new image. The second soft silicone orb completed the picture. Cheryl was already feeling quite feminine.

After successfully tucking beneath a panty girdle, pantyhose followed. Then a tight blue nylon skirt and a form fitting black top completed her transformation. Cheryl slipped on a pair of open-toe, ankle strap heels. She hadn't considered that she shouldn't have selected such high heels. She was always self-conscious with her height, so she had thought that higher was better. But held in the position her heels forced her legs to be in, her legs felt odd, and she felt unsteady. Cheryl had admired women walking in heels, but he had never realized what effort it took to do so in sky high heels. She tentatively stepped in front of the mirror again.

A big smile came over Cheryl's face. Even without makeup or the light blonde wig she had purchased, Cheryl looked like a girl. There was absolutely no doubt about it.

She took in her new form. Cheryl was sexy. Breasts that any girl would envy stood out prominently in the tight top. She felt self-conscious about her new bustline, but then she decided that all girls must feel that way at first. She would become accustomed to her boobs soon enough. At least so she thought.

The short tight skirt presented her legs in a manner she had seen on many girls. She decided that her youthful leggy look was sexy. She would have to be careful how she sat because a lady-like manner would be imperative in such a revealing skirt.

She knew that she was pulling it off. Cheryl was so excited with what she had accomplished that she quickly went for her wig. She carefully positioned it on her head in front of the mirror, before gently using a brush to fluff up the curly blonde locks that delightfully changed her appearance again. Her hands trembled with arousal while she applied a lavish coat of glossy pink lipstick. A touch of blush, a hint of eyeshadow, and Cheryl was nearly ready to go.

In her excitement, she almost forgot about the faux jewelry. She held her lavish hair aside, clipped gold hoop earrings on, and then added a black beaded necklace that dangled enticingly from her neck.

Her final step was to fill her new clutch bag with her student identification card and with the credit card that the University had provided her with. Things couldn't have gone any better!

She couldn't wait to try out her new self on the world. She quickly went to the front door and reached for the doorknob so she could make her entrance out into the real world. Then she froze, stopped cold with fear, her hand on the only way out of her apartment.

It dawned on her what she was doing. She was going outside dressed like a girl! Butterflies danced in her stomach. What if somebody recognized her? She could never live it down. They would laugh at her and they would humiliate her. She would be labelled sexually kinky. She would have to go back home in disgrace. She would never get to be with Robin or, for that matter, with any other girl.

She couldn't just walk out the door. She had to think about this a little bit further before she could summon the necessary courage to take the plunge.

Chapter 5. Easy-Peasy

It wasn't nearly as easy *psychologically* to become Cheryl as it had been to *dress* like Cheryl. In the safety of her apartment there was no risk. Going outside was a totally different story. It was daylight outside so she would be highly visible. She couldn't control things out there. The real world awaited her coming-out, but was Cheryl ready for the real world? She wasn't so sure.

There was still time to bring Daryl back. The boxes where she had put Daryl away were still there by the door. It would still be simple enough to change her mind. She could still play it safe.

But then there was Robin. Daryl could never have Robin, but at least Cheryl had a chance to get close to her. Or so Cheryl thought. She went back into her bedroom and sat on the chair at the dressing table fretting over what she should do next. She looked longingly at the lonely girl in the mirror wondering what was the best thing to do.

When she had conceived the scheme, it had seemed like such a simple thing to do. Change clothes and become best friends with Robin. Easy-peasy! But now, not so much.

In her mental struggle she finally realized something very important. She was on a strange college campus where nobody knew who she was. She really could go out without too much worrying. Since they didn't know who she was anyway, she actually had nothing to lose! Nothing except for Robin, and she didn't have Robin now anyway.

But deep inside, Cheryl was still the same shy, scared person that Daryl had always been. She was too frightened to go out into the world. She decided that she would turn back into Daryl and just forget the whole plan. But then what about Robin?

Her thoughts were interrupted. Was that a truck she heard outside of her apartment? She wasn't sure. She decided to ignore it.

Chapter 6. Moving Company

While Cheryl worried about her future, a truck had pulled up right in front of her apartment. Greg and Barry were ready to spring into action once again. This was their third college town of the day, so they had their scheme down perfectly.

It had all started for them the previous school year. Rent a truck, go into a college town, find one story apartments, and break in. Then grab everything they could, and then be on their way. Computers, tablets, and phones were worth a fortune these days. They had scored big last year, and this year was already shaping up to be a great year.

They posed as movers so that if they were seen nobody would think a thing about them. Their rental truck was already half filled with loot, and they were eager for more. Most students spent little time in their apartments the first week of school, so all they had to do was pop the door locks and help themselves.

Barry couldn't believe his luck when he tried the apartment door. It wasn't even locked! College students were so easy to take advantage of!

Barry and Greg stepped inside the apartment — Cheryl's apartment — and quickly scanned the room. Barry immediately noticed the boxes that were stacked near the front door.

"Greg, take those boxes out to the truck. They'll provide good cover. If anybody looks inside the truck, they will help us look like a real moving company."

Greg immediately began carrying boxes out the front door. Barry went over to the work desk. Jackpot! A laptop and a wallet filled with cash.

When Greg came back in after removing the first load of boxes, Barry beamed.

"Look at this, a laptop and a wallet filled with cash. Score!"

Greg smiled.

"Best take of the day."

Barry nodded.

"Hurry up, take the rest of the boxes and then we are out of here."

Greg picked up a few more boxes and headed out to the truck.

Back in her bedroom, Cheryl had heard the guys talking and temporarily forgot how she was dressed. She came out of the bedroom to find out who was in her apartment. She found Barry standing at the work desk holding her laptop and looking inside of Daryl's wallet.

"What are you doing in here?"

Her timid voice hardly alarmed Barry. He thought that the college coed in the skimpy little outfit was cute.

"Well hi there darling, I didn't realize that anyone was home. We're just moving things out for you."

Cheryl was confused.

"What do you mean? I just moved in."

Just then Greg walked back in the door. Barry nodded to Greg.

"The pretty girl here thinks that we're in the wrong place. Go back out to the truck and bring the paperwork in. Take the rest of the boxes with you. Oh, and bring some of that stuff to secure things in too."

Barry looked back at Cheryl.

"Don't you worry pretty girl, we'll get this all straightened out in just a minute."

Cheryl noticed that he was looking at Daryl's wallet. He had seen some of the identification inside. She was just about to say something when Barry spoke up again.

"We were hired by Daryl Meeks to take stuff here to another apartment. Just wait while Greg brings in the paperwork."

Cheryl couldn't very well say that *she* was Daryl Meeks, could she? Not dressed the way that she was dressed. So instead she just waited. Obviously their paperwork was wrong and this would get straightened out quickly enough.

Chapter 7. In A Bind

Cheryl couldn't believe what had happened to her. Hours had gone by since the movers had left and she was still helplessly secured to the chair in front of the work desk.

She had been so confused when the guys began to subdue her. They said that if she didn't struggle that they wouldn't hurt her. They said all they wanted to do was to buy time so that they could get away.

She didn't want to call for help because then she would have had to file a police report. She didn't want anybody checking on her identity. So she had cooperated. She had just submissively allowed them to chain her to the chair.

They had even thanked her for being so understanding. They said that normally they would have gagged her, but she had been so accommodating that they would spare her a gag. Instead, one of the guys had given her a deep wet kiss before they went out the door. Yuk!

She had been trying to wriggle free ever since she heard the sound of the truck drive away. But she was still hopelessly secured. She twisted and squirmed in a vain attempt to free herself.

She found being restrained like that to be erotic in a strange sort of way. She thought it to be the combination of her female attire along with her sense of complete helplessness. The whole episode helped her to feel more feminine. Anyway, feeling excited helped to make the time pass quicker while she struggled for freedom while she unwillingly played the role of damsel in distress.

Finally, with her last ounce of strength, she managed to free a hand. After that she was able to unravel the chain that had held her prisoner. She immediately looked around the room to take inventory of what was missing.

They had taken her laptop and the wallet that was next to it. So her cash was gone. They also took her cell phone. All of the boxes, with Daryl's clothing inside, were gone. Fortunately, they hadn't gone into her bedroom. At least she still had her purse with her student identification card and her credit card. It was still on the bed where she had left it.

Once the shock of being robbed wore off, another realization set in. She no longer had a choice to make. The decision had been made for her. When the boxes containing Daryl's clothes went out the door, her immediate future was determined for her. Daryl was gone for good.

Now she really *was* Cheryl Meeks.

Chapter 8. Cheryl Emerges

The good news was that the movers hadn't realized who she really was. They had treated her like a helpless girl, even going so far as to French kiss her on the mouth after they tied her up. One of the guys had grinned at her while he fondled her faux breasts. The whole episode had been extremely embarrassing. But it did prove one thing. Apparently she was *very* passable. Her new persona had even fooled the thieves. They had even spared her the trouble of getting rid of her guy clothes. The only real cost to her to find out had been a revolting kiss. The thought emboldened her to try out her new image. She decided to go outside and get a breath of fresh air to clear her head.

It had been light outside when the guys initially came in. Now it was dark out. With a deep breath, Cheryl opened the apartment door and she sheepishly stepped out into the night. She found that first step to be thrilling and filled with anticipation. Her heart fluttered and her face blushed with excitement. She needed to become comfortable with her Cheryl persona if she was going to venture out into the daylight. She decided that a quick walk around the block in the dark would help her to relax.

Cheryl didn't get very far before she realized that she had made a mistake. One of the Frat houses was holding a big party so there were many guys out walking towards the party. They immediately started hitting on her, offering to accompany her to the party. Cheryl was certainly *not* ready for *that*! So she quickly retreated back to her apartment.

Once she was safely inside again, she decided that she would stay inside until her first class began. She spent the next couple of days refining her makeup, practicing her feminine walk, and practicing how to sit like a lady.

So when the day of her first class arrived, Cheryl was more confident. Thankfully, when she stepped outside, none of the other students paid any attention to her. When she entered her first class, nobody even looked up. She was surprised, but definitely relieved.

Even better, she saw Robin sitting in the back of the room all by herself. Cheryl summoned up all of her courage and sat down right next to her. She nervously introduced herself. It was the first time that she had ever spoken to the beautiful girl of her dreams.

"Hi my name is Cheryl. Do you mind if I sit here?"

Robin looked pleased.

"Absolutely. I'm new here. I don't have a single friend on campus. Nobody wants to even talk with me."

Cheryl smiled. This was perfect!

After that, things went well. Over the next few days they attended every lecture together. Cheryl had made sure that their schedules matched up perfectly. Getting to know Robin was easy. Robin freely shared everything about herself with Cheryl.

Cheryl was ecstatic with the quick progress that she had made. Then the first big problem came up. Robin needed money. She had to work in order to stay on campus. She talked Cheryl into applying for a job at the same place that she wanted to work at. It was a tawdry hangout called *Tits N Ass*.

Most students didn't want to work on campus. So the chances of being hired were good. The problem was that Cheryl didn't really want to become a waitress at the tacky bar and grill that most students frequented. It wasn't the sort of place that Cheryl was comfortable with. How could she possibly be? Any place called *Tits N Ass* would be uncomfortable for any girl to work, let alone for a faux girl like her to work.

Chapter 9. Tits N Ass Girls

Tits N Ass was a local bar and grill where food and drink weren't the only two of the tempting things on the menu. Their motto of *look but don't touch* was not considered to be a rule, only a loose guideline.

Guys frequented the place because it was a great way to meet girls close up and personal. Robin wanted to work at *Tits N Ass* because she wanted to meet boys so for her it was a good match. She thought that the revealing *Tits N Ass* uniform all the waitresses wore gave her the best chance to attract a guy with her alluring feminine features. That was the same reason that Cheryl *didn't* want to work there. But if Robin wanted to work there, then Cheryl knew that she would have to work there too.

Cheryl was appalled at the revealing attire. The uniform was a tight-fitting, long sleeve, nylon thong leotard. The form-fitting garment had a V-neckline that nicely drew attention to her breasts and presented them perfectly for amorous eyes. Cheryl was glad that she had selected the D breast forms because she knew that she most likely could never get the job with anything less than that.

The sexy outfit was obviously designed to accentuate female breasts and buttocks. It scarcely covered enough front and rear to be legal, with only the bare minimum of skin covered below the waist. All of the girls had their pubic hair shaved off. Not because of choice, but rather out of necessity. Cheryl was glad that she had done so too.

But because the outfit conformed perfectly to female bodies, *all* of the girls' plentiful assets were boldly displayed for the pleasure of the patrons. Any girl wearing such an outfit might as well have been screaming that she wanted sex.

The position was clearly less about waitressing and more about objectifying the women who were strutting their stuff for the customers. It was an attraction even better than food and drink that most males couldn't resist. Most likely, that's why the place was frequented by so many eligible guys.

Cheryl didn't really want any part of the tawdry outfit or of the work, but it was far too early to tell Robin the truth. She hadn't even started preparing her for such an unexpected pronouncement. So she went along with the idea to apply for a job at *Tits N Ass*. The interview consisted of the applicants donning a work uniform, complete with stiletto heels to show off their rear, and then parading in front of the bar crowd. If there was a positive reaction, then the girls would become *Tits N Ass* waitresses. It was juvenile, and humiliating, but it was the way they selected their waitresses.

Cheryl was glad the uniform didn't show any more cleavage than it already did. Her breast forms were still safely undercover, even if her bottom wasn't. Her tucking job and tiny penis allowed her to get away with the lower portion of the outfit so long as hands didn't roam too far.

Both girls were summarily paraded past the bar holding a tray of drinks, where guys showed absolutely no respect for them. They made rude comments like "nice rack" and "how about a fucking good time." Catcalls and bottom pinching were also part of the embarrassing humiliation. One of the guys called Cheryl a "blonde bimbo." Another guy slapped Robin on her bottom. The girls needed the job so they willingly accepted the abuse.

Having been thoroughly objectified, both girls were

immediately hired.

Training, what little there was, was done on the job. The girls were told that anything goes in the bar and grill, at least within reason. They were not allowed to resist customer advances, and they were to report anything outrageous to the manager on duty. Oh, and between dodging wayward advances, they were also to serve food and drink.

Things went fairly well during the training period and the first few days on the job. Cheryl did cringe every time she slipped into her uniform. She had to be careful not to allow her faux breasts to give away their secret. With the right bra, she managed to pull off the ruse. Tucking also had to be done carefully or else she would be outed.

Robin took a different view of the sexual objectification. Robin said that she thought that the attention was flattering. While Robin seemed to be enjoying her nightly fondling, Cheryl was not happy at all. Not only was she being ogled by guys, she had to endure watching Robin being groped. It was not easy to stand by while the girl he adored was treated like that.

Things got out of hand the second Friday that they worked. Cheryl was bringing out a tray of clam chowder soup to her table when she noticed a guy harassing Robin. Robin was holding a tray of drinks at the time. A guy was feeling her up while she carefully balanced her tray filled with adult beverages.

Cheryl couldn't handle watching her girlfriend being mauled like that. She completely lost control, and in a move she later regretted, she walked over to the table where Robin was being fondled.

Cheryl came up behind the rude customer. Then, in one swift motion, she unceremoniously dumped a substantial amount of clam chowder over the head of the guy who was harassing Robin.

Perhaps emboldened by the actions of her new best friend, Robin asked the customer if he would like a drink with his soup. Then Robin followed up the clam chowder shower by pouring a couple of beers over his head for good measure.

The stunned soup guy recovered his senses and then turned to confront his attacker. When he saw that it was a girl, there was nothing that he could do about it since he couldn't very well hit a girl.

He had been completely humiliated by two girls! The whole place erupted with laughter while another *Tits N Ass* girl came over with a towel to help him get cleaned up.

It was an evening that went down in *Tits N Ass* lore. The story would be retold by other waitresses for years afterwards. Cheryl and Robin became the heroic waitresses who had finally confronted a customer the way all of the girls had always wanted to do.

Both girls were immediately fired.

Chapter 10. Downhill

At first the girls laughed about losing their jobs at *Tits N Ass*. They said it was no great loss. After all, even though the tips were outrageously good, the customers constantly groped them. Both girls had routinely come home after their shift with red bottoms from all of the bottom pinching that went on at *Tits N Ass*. They had put up with it because the tips were good, even if it was terribly humiliating.

But the reality was that they had needed the money in order to live on campus. It was Robin who came up with the idea that saved the day. Since she had a two-bedroom apartment, while Cheryl only had a one-bedroom apartment, why not have Cheryl move in with her? That way they could share expenses.

"Cheryl, why don't you move in with me? I have an extra bedroom and that way we could spend more time together."

Cheryl couldn't believe her good fortune. She had become good friends with Robin, but never in her wildest dreams did she think that she would be able to live with her. Up to this point, Cheryl had been satisfied just to bask in the glow of Robin's presence. She lived in awe of her bubbly personality and her quick wit. In her eyes, Robin was a goddess. Living with Robin would be a dream come true. Robin interrupted her thoughts.

"Cheryl? Cheryl? Are you still there?"

"Oh, sorry, just thinking about the possibilities."

 Well, are you going to move in with me?"

Cheryl smiled.

"Of course I will!"

So it was settled. Things moved quickly after that. In just a couple of days Cheryl had all of her things in her new bedroom. The girls became even closer together than before.

Of course the relationship was completely nonsexual. How else could it be? Cheryl was presenting herself like a girlfriend and Robin was enjoying every minute with her new best friend.

They did everything together. They went to class together, they shopped together, and they ate their meals together. Robin showed Cheryl how to do a French manicure so they could do each other's nails. They did facials together and Robin even plucked and shaped Cheryl's eyebrows for her. She had said that they were *"far too bushy for a pretty girl to have brows like that!"*

Cheryl was living the dream of a lifetime. The only problem was that she realized that the closer they became, the more difficult it would be to tell Robin the truth. How could she possibly explain that she had deceived her in order to get closer to her?

By mid-terms the two girls were inseparable. They were also flat broke. They both agreed that they had to do something quick or else they would soon be evicted from their apartment.

Robin had heard that the local hotel, *The Aterberry*, was hiring housekeeping maids. She really didn't want to work at the hotel, but there weren't any other jobs available. A girl has to do what a girl has to do. Reluctantly, Cheryl went with her to apply for jobs.

Chapter 11. Hotel Maids

The Aterberry was a posh hotel where wealthy elites stayed when visiting their college student. They had a longstanding tradition of the best fine impeccable service that money could buy. The work was demanding, which was why the housekeeping staff often turned over. So they always had the need for more chambermaids.

It was in the office of Madam Miriam Stricklin, head of housekeeping, where Cheryl was interviewed for the chambermaid position. Robin had been interviewed first, and she had already landed a position.

While Cheryl waited outside Madam Stricklin's office, Robin had been interviewed and awarded a position. She had left Madam Stricklin's office holding her new uniform with a big smile on her face.

The Aterberry maid uniforms were both practical and traditional. They were simple black dresses that fell just above the knee, with a white flourish at the sleeves and at the collar. It was the frilly white lace apron with matching headdress that made the uniforms special. Both were hardly functional. They were each designed simply to give the maids a feminine flare while they went about their business.

Cheryl wasn't sure if Robin landing a position was good news, or not. Becoming a hotel maid wasn't particularly appealing, but she was willing to give it a try. She timidly entered Madam Stricklin's office when the head of housekeeping beckoned her in.

Madam Stricklin was a rugged no-nonsense woman who

expected the very best out of her employees. Madam Stricklin sat behind her desk appearing very much to be a woman in charge. There was no chair in the office for Cheryl to sit, so she stood in front of the matronly woman like a meek little girl waiting for her decision. Madam Stricklin looked Cheryl up and down before she spoke.

"You certainly don't look like maid material, girl. Why should I employ you?"

Cheryl was taken aback by such an abrupt question. She froze for a moment before she finally came out with her answer.

"Because, Madam Stricklin, I desperately need this position and I will do anything to please you in your service."

Madam Stricklin raised an eyebrow.

"Anything?"

"Yes Madam, *anything*."

If there was one attribute that Meriam Stricklin looked for in a maid, it was the willingness to do whatever it took to get the job done. Clients of *The Aterberry* could be quite demanding. It was the reason that turnover was so high. She really didn't want to be bothered with trivial matters. She just expected her maids to handle everything on their own.

Madam Stricklin smiled.

"You're hired."

Chapter 12. Mom's Lesson

Though Cheryl had put it out of her mind, and she certainly didn't want to ever admit it, even to herself, this wasn't the first time that she would work like a real maid.

Right after his Father had run off with a younger woman, Daryl had been left with his Mother and sister. His Father got a new wife, his Mother got the house.

It was the summer just after sophomore year in high school. Daryl had left a mess in the kitchen after eating a snack.

Daryl's Mother, Dianna, worked as a maid at a local hotel. She had just returned home from work and she was exhausted. She was definitely not in a good mood. It had been a particularly stressful week at the hotel with a rowdy group of physicians attending a conference. They had left quite a mess behind.

That evening Dianna had invited several of her fellow maids over for a relaxing evening with wine, cheese, and conversation. Dianna was annoyed at Daryl for the mess that he had made in the kitchen and she told him to clean it up.

Without giving it much thought, Daryl had quipped that his Mother was dressed like a maid so maybe she should clean it up herself. Naturally, that set Dianna off, and she yelled at Daryl.

"Oh, you think that *I'm* a maid? *Oh Really?* Maybe *you'd* like to be a maid for a while and see how it feels!"

Of course Daryl objected. But it didn't matter to Dianna. After a serious argument, Daryl went over Dianna's knee for an attitude adjustment.

Daryl's older sister Linda heard the commotion and came into the kitchen just in time to help out. Dianna told Linda to take Daryl's pants down. So with a giggle Linda pulled down Daryl's pants. She giggled even more when her Mother told her to yanked his underwear down too. Dianna then had Daryl wait in the juvenile position over her lap while she had Linda fetch the paddle. The wooden instrument hadn't been put to use since Daryl was five years old. She also had Linda bring a pair of panties, one of her bras, and pantyhose for use after Daryl's spanking.

When Linda returned, she enjoyed watching with great amusement, while Dianna lectured Daryl and turned his bottom a bright shade of heated red.

"You will respect women!"

The paddle made a loud noise when smacked against Daryl's bottom.

"We'll see who the maid is in this household!"

Another loud thwack echoed in the kitchen.

"You'll regret being such a brazen *hussy*!"

Smack!

At first Daryl pleaded for mercy. While Dianna continued to apply the paddle, he kicked his legs in an attempt to lessen the blows until he grudgingly gave in to her female authority. The final spanks were applied with tears falling and Daryl limply positioned over Dianna's lap in full surrender.

He thought that the worst was over. But for Daryl, his lesson
was just beginning. His Mother would see to that.

Chapter 13. Mom's Maid

After his spanking, Daryl stood in front of his Mother, appearing quite contrite. When Dianna had Linda remove his shirt, he knew what was coming. He only made a lame attempt to protest—his Mother held the paddle in hand at the ready.

"Please Mom, I didn't mean it…"

Dianna was not listening. She took the bra from Linda and had Daryl put his hands through the straps. Then Daryl suffered the indignity of having his older sister clip his very first bra in place from behind him.

Dianna wasn't satisfied just putting him in a bra. She noted that the D cups looked "unfulfilled" on him.

"Linda, bring a few pairs of my old stockings to fill those out. Our maid should have a proper bust."

When Linda returned, Daryl's older sister padded out his bra. By the time she finished, his full-figure D cups were quite full.

Panties followed. It was only after Linda pulled them up on her brother that she noticed that he had a full-blown hard-on. She gave a little giggle when she pointed out his erection to her Mother.

"Mom, I think he's enjoying himself!"

Dianna smiled.

"Good because he's going to be wearing those clothes for

quite a while."

Linda told Daryl how to put his pantyhose on. He sat down and struggled, but eventually the pantyhose were smoothed up to his knees. Then she had him stand and pull them the rest of the way into place. While he stood red-faced in front of his Mother and sister, Dianna took her own maid uniform off and gave it to Daryl. She stood quite confidently in front of him dressed only in her undergarments.

"Put this on right now!"

Daryl knew from the tone of her voice that he had best not protest. Dianna observed, stripped down to her own lingerie, while Daryl obediently dressed. He couldn't believe that his Mother was putting him into female clothing.

He glanced a few times at her while he reluctantly buttoned up the dress. He had never before seen a woman in just her undergarments. He found her curves to be quite lovely. He had never seen his Mother in such a state of undress and he found himself staring at her breasts.

Dianna had been working all day long in the maid uniform. Daryl found that her scent was all over the dress, including her fragrant perfume. He fumbled with the apron before putting the lace cap on his head that the maids at the hotel where his Mother worked were required to wear.

Dianna stood back with an approving smile. It was all the more satisfying for her because the uniform had *Housekeeping* embroidered on it in bright white thread. She had always wanted a maid of her own!

"There you go *Cheryl*. A few more modifications and you'll be ready to work."

That was the first time that Daryl became Cheryl—it was the name that his Mother had first called him that day. Dianna looked at Linda.

"Take *Cheryl* to your room and make her up while I get dressed. I want her to look like a proper lady. I'll be there in a few minutes."

Linda giggled with glee. It's not very often that a girl gets to turn her little brother into a housemaid but she was about to get to do it. She couldn't wait to tell all of her friends.

"Follow me *Cheryl*."

Cheryl followed meekly behind her older sister. When they arrived at Linda's bedroom she had the maid sit down at her vanity.

To Cheryl, it seemed like Linda fussed over her for hours, though it wasn't nearly that long. She did have time to pluck a few stray eyebrows, use foundation, blush, eyeshadow, and a luscious pink lipstick on her blushing maid. For a final touch, Linda had an old pair of black patent low heels that fit Cheryl perfectly. Just when she finished up, Dianna came into the room to check on progress.

"Linda you did a splendid job. Cheryl looks very cute. A suitable girl for the job if ever there was one. Time to put her to work. Cheryl, see to the mess in the kitchen."

Cheryl had no choice. Her bottom still stung from her spanking and her Mom was in no mood to argue. Cheryl quickly went off to the kitchen to clean up. She could hear her sister laughing behind her back in her bedroom when she left.

Chapter 14. Company Comes

Cheryl thought that cleaning up the kitchen while in uniform would put an end to her punishment. She had learned her lesson. But instead, Dianna put her to work preparing a cheese tray along with fresh fruits, vegetables with dip, and other finger foods.

Still thinking the worst was over, Cheryl was horrified when Dianna told her that she would be answering the door when guests arrived and that she would also be serving for the evening. "After all," her Mother said, "She was the maid!"

The first few guests in the door hardly paid any attention to Cheryl. They simply thought that she was one of the hotel maids that they didn't know. It wasn't until all of the guests had arrived that one of the ladies asked who the new maid was.

Dianna made no attempt to shield Cheryl from excruciating humiliation. In fact, she deliberately applied it and enjoyed every moment of it.

"Oh that's *Cheryl*. She's my new daughter and my new housemaid. She used to be my son Daryl, but she was so envious of us! She wanted to be a maid, and she insisted, so I let her try it out for tonight. Personally, I think that she's a keeper."

The ladies took another long look at Cheryl before bursting out into a chorus of laughter. Cheryl was so convincing that they would have never guessed the true identity of the maid had Dianna not mentioned it. The announcement set off a night long string of teasing Cheryl for being a "very fine young woman" with a "bright housekeeping future." All of the ladies commented on what a pretty girl she was.

Surprisingly, even with all of the teasing, Cheryl did a decent job of serving the women that evening. Once the ladies settled in, they simply treated her the way they would treat a waitress at a diner. Cheryl poured wine, served finger food, and she even cleaned up when they left. Oddly, she found the whole experience to be rather erotic. She had never been in such close proximity to so many pretty women before and she found her uniform to be a real turn on.

The thing was, Dianna appreciated the help. So it didn't take much convincing from Linda for her to decide that Cheryl was going to spend the whole summer as their personal housekeeper.

Like serving female guests wasn't humiliating enough, that next day Cheryl's Mother put her back in uniform. Then she took her around the house explaining all of her new chores. Cheryl's sister Linda followed gleefully along while Dianna explained things to the new maid.

Cheryl had to be told how to sort clothes for washing. She had no idea how to turn on the washing machine. Similarly, operating the dryer was a whole new experience.

Cheryl could still remember standing in her maid uniform in front of the laundry tub for the first time. Her Mother watched intently while Cheryl was instructed how to properly wash out and scent woman's lingerie. Each garment had to be softly placed in the tub and lightly cleaned before being rinsed out. Cheryl was told to be extremely careful with all of the lace and finery of the feminine garments.

After proper washing, Cheryl had to hang lingerie to dry in

the bathroom. Dianna made sure that Cheryl knew that was a special concession she was making just for the dignity of her maid. If Cheryl didn't wash things properly, she would have to hang lingerie outside on the line. *That* was a humiliation that Cheryl didn't want to ever experience. It was bad enough that after that first day of laundry duty, Linda would occasionally tease Cheryl by calling her Panty Girl.

The lesson continued. The new maid would dust and vacuum on a regular basis. The maid learned how to prepare and serve basic meals. She would load and unload the dishwasher and clean pots and pans by hand.

Linda was amused when her Mother taught the maid how to wash floors. After carefully sweeping the floors, Cheryl had to hand wash them down on her hands and knees. Cheryl had to lift her dress a bit in order to kneel down and that just added to her embarrassment.

That day Linda was assigned to watch over the maid while she dutifully washed all of the tile floors. Linda was happy to be of help. She stood close to the maid to observe her while she did the job. It forced Cheryl to crawl along while she worked at her sister's feet. It gave Linda the wonderful sensation of having her sissy brother grovel at her feet.

After that humiliating day, Dianna had Linda further feminize the maid. Dianna gave Cheryl all of her second-hand maid uniforms so that she had a wardrobe of her own for the summer. Real breast forms replaced the wadded-up nylons to give the maid a realistic womanly bust complete with protruding nipples. Linda handed down some of her worn lingerie. Linda worked with Cheryl on feminine grooming habits. Cheryl had to shave her legs and underarms just like a girl. That summer Dianna also had Cheryl grow her hair out. Then she had Linda take her to the salon so she could have it styled into a more feminine cut.

That was one of the reasons that Daryl appeared even more feminine when he returned to school the next fall. Linda thought that the feminine cut looked cute on him so he had to keep it. Combined with his eyebrows being plucked, he really did look like a girl.

At Dianna's suggestion, Linda also took Cheryl for a manicure and pedicure session. Girls keep their nails pretty! Linda put Cheryl into a cute pink jumpsuit for the visit. Cheryl wasn't nearly as uncomfortable getting her nails done as she had been getting her hair styled. At that point, she was so feminine appearing that all the ladies at the salon just thought that she was another female client. None of the ladies paid any particular attention to her.

When the technician finished with Cheryl's nails, she had pretty pink fingernails with extensions, along with matching toenails. After that she had to be careful not to run her stockings with her longer nails when she dressed.

Cheryl spent that summer, and the summer after that, dressed like a housemaid doing all of the household chores for her Mother and her sister. During the school year, Cheryl had to change into uniform when she came home after class.

That second summer Linda began dating. Cheryl was taught how to do Linda's makeup and how to style her hair. That was how Cheryl learned how to properly apply makeup, mist perfume, and how to braid hair. Linda loved the attention and the perk of having her own maid.

Cheryl's Mother also took advantage of Cheryl's new skills. By then she was also dating so Cheryl would tend to her before she went out for the evening.

For Cheryl, assisting her Mother and sister became routine. She was even asked to help her Mother and sister dress. Since she helped both Dianna and Linda to dress, it didn't take long for Cheryl to become accustomed to seeing them in various stages of undress. She appreciated being in the company of women and she didn't want to spoil it by becoming rude. So she understood she needed to control her lewd thoughts. That was also how she learned not to gape at a naked woman. She was told by Dianna that was not at all polite for a maid to do so.

That was also how Cheryl discovered the different types of bras. Linda wore balconette bras that enhanced her bust. Dianna wore full-figured bras for support. Cheryl also learned never to criticize or even ask about a woman's measurements or weight. Cheryl learned that women were sensitive about these things, particularly their breasts. It only took one trip over Dianna's lap to learn *that* lesson.

After she was dressed like a maid, and began to act like one, Cheryl's role in the household changed considerably. For Linda, Cheryl wasn't quite a sister, and she certainly wasn't a brother. She was more like a helpful live-in maid. For Dianna, Cheryl became a young maid who needed tutoring in the art of domestic chores. Both Dianna and Linda enjoyed having a maid in their home.

When Linda brought her friends over to visit, the first time they laughed and giggled at what had become of Linda's brother. Linda regaled them with the story of Cheryl's arousal the first time she was paddled. They teased him unmercifully about wearing a maid uniform. But after that they just became familiar with Linda's maid and they just treated her like she was the real thing.

Had Dianna not met a gentleman, most likely Cheryl would have continued to be her housemaid. It was only after Linda moved out and Dianna met someone and moved out of the house that Daryl left his uniform behind and was returned to his Father. That was when he first met his step Mother. He only knew her for a short time before finally being put out of the house to go to college.

Daryl had in fact occasionally fantasized about becoming a feminized maid again for a pretty girl. He had found the experience to be sexually fulfilling and the fantasy to be erotic. The opportunity had simply not presented itself, so his thoughts had remained tucked away in his imagination.

So while Daryl had reluctantly become Cheryl on campus, she had already spent considerable time posing as a girl. She also had housekeeping experience, having already been put to the apron once before. She had only been hesitant to assume her female identity because she was on campus and she was not safely at home with her Mother and sister to watch over her. She was still uncertain of herself outside the safety of her own home.

But the fact remained that he found dressing up like a girl to be quite enticing.

Chapter 15. The Aterberry

The Aterberry was serious about their employees. Things had to be done The Aterberry way. So Robin and Cheryl were both trained how to be proper Aterberry maids. One wouldn't think that there was a correct method of cleaning toilets, but both had to become proficient at The Aterberry way of doing so.

Working at *The Aterberry* was pure drudgery. Room after room of endless sheet changing, dusting, vacuuming, and bathroom cleanup. The clients were snooty snobs. People with big money can be like that.

Robin was supervised on the third floor by a charming maid named Mary who would occasionally check on her work and compliment her on a job well done. The delightful woman was a pleasure to work with. Robin didn't have a single complaint.

Cheryl, on the other hand, was supervised on the fourth floor by a dreadful woman named Hilda. The woman followed her around while she worked, constantly nagging at her for her sloppy work. She made Cheryl feel like she was completely incompetent.

Cheryl was helpless to do anything about the situation. All she could do was try to act like a perfect Aterberry maid. She would lower her eyes and allow the woman to heap criticism on her.

It was at The Aterberry where Robin met Trevor Tolworth. Trevor was a partner in a successful tech company and he was relocating in order to be closer to the business. He was staying at The Aterberry until he could procure adequate housing. Robin had entered his room to clean, and she found him sleeping nude in his bed. Apparently Trevor had a rather raucous night out on the town and he was still sleeping it off.

Instead of immediately leaving the room, Robin had stood and stared at the naked man. It was her first encounter with a nude male. His slight body was well toned and he seemed to be everything that a woman could desire.

Robin was lost in her dreamy notions when Trevor woke up. He leered hungrily at the pretty vision in the maid uniform who was taken by his naked body.

Robin was spellbound when he stood up and approached her. She stayed motionless when he grasped her by her shoulders and pulled her close. His ardor was clearly evident, fully gorged and pressed up against her body, straining for relief. His hungry tongue delved into her mouth while she stayed frozen in his manly grip.

His hands roamed underneath her freshly pressed dressed. His fingertips found the waistband of her pantyhose. He was going to take her, and there was absolutely nothing she could do about it. She returned his kiss with a longing passion that had waited for just this moment.

Trevor certainly had a thing for maids. He would have taken her right then and there had there not been a knock at the door. Mary had come by to check on Robin.

Even though their embrace was interrupted, Trevor was not to be denied. He arrogantly ordered Robin to meet him in the hotel lounge after her shift ended so that he could get to know her better. Robin meekly complied.

Chapter 16. Robin's Boyfriend

One thing led to another. Robin had a new boyfriend! Trevor was everything that a girl like Robin could possibly want. He was fine featured, rich, and charming. They dated for months while Robin surrendered to his charms.

Of course she would tease him and they would make-out like horny teens in his hotel room. But Robin wouldn't fully surrender her womanhood to him. She told him that would only happen if he married her.

Cheryl was stunned the night Robin came home wearing a shiny new engagement ring. Trevor had proposed marriage and Robin had gleefully accepted. To add insult to injury, Robin immediately asked Cheryl to be her maid of honor.

This was not what Cheryl had expected to happen. Naturally she accepted the honor. What choice did she really have?

Trevor wanted to hold a small wedding, and he wanted to hold it as soon as possible. Robin laughed about that. Apparently Trevor was pressuring Robin to make love. Robin had said that sex was off limits until they were married. Soon after he had proposed.

While Robin was excited about her marriage, Cheryl pointed out that sex alone was not a good reason to get married. For obvious reasons, Cheryl never liked Trevor, and now she was even more suspicious of him.

Nevertheless, Cheryl accompanied Robin to the local bridal shop where both girls were fitted for the wedding. Robin made a glowing bride in a flattering white satin and lace sheath gown that brought out the very best in her figure. Trevor had insisted that she find something sexy and her dress was perfect. She beamed with excitement when she saw herself in the mirror for the first time.

Cheryl couldn't help but notice how the form fitting wedding gown was tight all the way to Robin's ankles. She wondered how brides were able to walk in such a tight dress. At least the bridesmaid dress that Cheryl had gave her enough room to walk comfortably.

Cheryl was fitted with a flowing pink satin evening dress that tightly hugged her body. Cheryl enjoyed the fine satin fabric of her bridesmaid dress. She had never worn such a wonderful dress before. She found herself thinking that pretending to be a girl had turned out to be a fantastic idea.

The saleslady smiled her glowing approval of both ladies. She even noted that both the bride and her maid of honor wore the same size dress. She smiled when she said that was unusual.

Both girls were happy with their choices.

Chapter 17. Issues

With the wedding day set, and dresses back in the apartment at the ready, the excitement continued to build. It all came crashing down when Trevor's true motivation came to light.

Robin came home that evening with her blouse torn, and her panties in tatters. Her lips were bruised, and tears flowed freely down her cheeks. Trevor had tried to rape her!

Cheryl gave Robin a big hug while her best friend relayed what had happened that awful evening.

Trevor had insisted on "trying her out" before the wedding. When she resisted, he had simply helped himself. He dragged Robin onto his bed and pinned her down on her back. He tore her blouse open and unclipped her bra. Robin tried to scream for help, but he covered her mouth with rough kisses. After he lifted her skirt, he tore her panties off with one hungry swipe of his hand.

He mauled her like a hungry animal. He paid no attention to her pleas to resist temptation. During the struggle, Robin realized that Trevor simply wanted her for sex. He had absolutely no respect for her. Hardly the basis for a lifelong commitment!

Robin put up a valiant struggle. Had Robin not had the sense to knee him in the groin, she most certainly would have been raped. Instead, her ardent fiancé howled in painful agony. The well-placed blow ended what would have been a terrible violation of her most intimate place. But she was saving herself for the man of her dreams, not for a lout who only wanted her for his selfish sexual gratification. She would not submit to that!

While Trevor tried to rub off the pain, Robin got up and ran to the door. The last thing that she did was take her engagement ring off and then she threw it at him.

Just like that, the wedding was off.

While Cheryl never wanted Robin to experience such a thing, secretly she was happy. With Trevor out of the way, marrying Robin was still a possibility.

After Robin changed out of her tattered outfit, Cheryl consoled her the way only a trusted friend could. They shared a glass of wine while Robin recounted every sordid detail.

If there was one thing in the world that Robin could count on, it was her girlfriend Cheryl.

Chapter 18. Changes

Robin's experience with Trevor changed her attitude towards boys. She decided that she would never, ever, let herself be taken advantage of again. Further, she no longer wanted to go out with guys. She swore them off forever. She decided to change her appearance in order to fend them off.

Her new outlook became apparent the following week. She took off all of her jewelry and put it back into her jewelry box. She didn't apply her makeup like she did every morning. Then she took a trip to the salon and had her hairstyle changed. Her new boyish cut drastically transformed her appearance. She followed the trip to the stylist with a clothes shopping trip.

She returned to the apartment that afternoon carrying several packages. She had completely altered her wardrobe. Now she was wearing men's slacks, a men's button up shirt, and guy's shoes. Underneath, she wore a minimizer bra that considerably toned down her figure.

Robin's transition was radical to say the least. At first Cheryl didn't even recognize her. Robin's expression of fiery determination told it all. Cheryl approached her cautiously.

"Robin, what happened? Why did you change like that?"

"I'm tired of guys who treat me like dirt. I don't want any part of them. I didn't want them looking at me like I'm some sort of sex object anymore."

Cheryl couldn't help but smile.

"I can see that. What do they call that look — guy repellant?"

That immediately changed the mood. Both girls laughed. Robin spoke next.

"Maybe I overdid it a bit. But you know, I kind of like it. There is a certain amount of freedom in not being a helpless girl."

"What about your job at the hotel?"

Robin smiled.

"I couldn't very well go to work looking like this, could I? I wouldn't fit The Aterberry image. So I quit. I won't make another bed, vacuum another rug, or sanitize another bathroom. Not *ever* again!"

It was quite a change, to say the least. Now Cheryl would have to pay the rent on the apartment. Hopefully Robin would land another position quickly.

Cheryl couldn't help but feel the irony of what Robin had done to herself. Robin could now pass for a guy, while Cheryl was already passing for a girl. What a strange world!

Over the next few weeks Cheryl became accustomed to the new Robin. Her clothes seemed to change her temperament. She became more demanding and more assertive. She seemed confident and more authoritative. Yet Cheryl found that despite her change in appearance, along with her new attitude, she still felt the same way about Robin that she did before. If anything, Cheryl found Robin to be even more attractive than ever. There was something about her quick wit and those pretty eyes that Cheryl just couldn't resist.

She was still madly in love with the woman of her dreams.

Chapter 19. Working Girls

At the end of the school semester, Robin's extraordinary grades earned her a paid internship position in the exclusive work/study program. She was excited about her new work.

It was difficult to hold down a part-time job while attending college, but Robin managed to do it. After all, she could use the money and it was great experience. So things were really looking up for Robin.

For Cheryl, things didn't go quite so well. She never really had an interest in computer science other than an interest in Robin. Cheryl failed every one of her classes. So she was forced to drop out of college. She had to accept that she was destined to continue being a maid working at The Aterberry hotel if she wanted to stay with Robin.

Cheryl fit in well at The Aterberry. She could really relate to the other maids. Cheryl never really liked being around guys so she was happy to continue on at the hotel with the other girls even if Robin no longer worked there.

Cheryl did get the occasional harassment from male hotel patrons. She decided that it must be something about the maid uniform, though she really wasn't sure. She brushed them aside without too much thought. She was definitely careful to avoid Trevor's hotel suite. He was still staying there and she had no intention of running into him.

Things did change back at the apartment. Robin's schedule was far more demanding so she came home later than Cheryl. Since Cheryl was dressed like a maid anyway, Robin decided that Cheryl could do all of the cooking, cleaning, and laundry.

Cheryl simply couldn't say no to Robin, so her position in the household was firmed up.

Though Robin was only working part-time, she essentially became the head of the household. Her position was evident to anyone who happened to visit because Cheryl looked and acted like a hired maid.

For Cheryl, it was what she had wanted. She had found a way to stay close to the woman of her dreams, no questions asked. The only problem was that she wanted to be more than just Robin's maid. She wanted to be romantically involved with the beautiful woman.

Chapter 20. Daryl Returns

Robin's experience with Trevor caused Cheryl to rethink everything that she was doing with Robin. That was when she came up with a scheme to introduce Robin to Daryl. It was a Saturday, when Robin was at home, that Cheryl said that she was going to work. She left the apartment in her maid uniform. She was careful to wear her sneakers instead of the heels that she normally wore to the hotel.

Cheryl stopped at a store and picked up guy jeans, a plaid shirt, and a small suitcase. Then, when no one was looking, she stepped into a unisex bathroom. There, she changed clothes back into Daryl. She stuffed the maid uniform, her wig, and her jewelry into the suitcase and then quickly washed her makeup off before leaving the room. Daryl tried to arrange his hair more like a guy but he hadn't realized how much it had grown out. He had been covering it with his wig so he hadn't noticed how long it had grown. He did the best he could with it.

Daryl returned to Robin's apartment and knocked on the door. Robin answered.

"Hi, I'm Daryl, Cheryl's twin brother. I was just passing through town and I decided to stop by. Is she at home?"

Robin was surprised. Cheryl had never mentioned a twin brother.

"No, she's not here. Would you care to come in?"

"Yes, please."

Daryl walked in and sat down on the small sofa. Once Robin got a good look at Daryl she was immediately suspicious. Daryl had his eyebrows shaped the same way she had shaped Cheryl's. Daryl hadn't thought about his nails — they still looked feminine. The way Daryl had come inside the apartment, Daryl seemed almost too comfortable. She also noticed that he had a touch of lipstick left on his lips. That was the final telltale sign.

She decided that Cheryl was playing a game. She decided to put an end to it before it got out of hand.

"Cheryl, I know that is you. What's this all about?"

Daryl couldn't believe how quickly Robin had seen through the charade.

Daryl couldn't help himself any longer. He broke down, and told Robin the whole story. He poured his heart out to the woman he adored. While Robin listened attentively, Daryl even told her that he loved her and that he wanted to marry her.

Robin was stunned, to say the least. She had been living with a guy all of this time and she didn't even know it! Her first instinct was to be angry. Her initial impulse was to throw Daryl out the door and never see him again. But she saw how serious her best friend was so she tried not to show her anger.

Instead she stayed silent while Daryl confessed everything that he had done in order to be near to her. Robin decided that Daryl was cute and that perhaps she could work with the situation.

When Daryl finally finished, Robin just stared silently at him for a few minutes before she spoke. Daryl fidgeted nervously waiting to hear what Robin was going to do.

Robin was somewhat familiar with boys who liked to dress up like girls. The girls at *Tit's N Ass* had talked about such things. They were so dismayed at the callousness of the patrons that they longed for more sensitive guys. A girl can only put up with so much groping!

Sheila, one of the more experienced waitresses, spoke about crossdressers and sissy maids. These were both guys who dressed up in female clothing. Sheila had said that there was a difference between the two.

Crossdressers, also called transvestites, were straight males who received pleasure from dressing up in female clothing. They liked to dress and make themselves up so that they could pretend to be female. They also tended to have a male side that they would always show to the world. They were sexually attracted to women even when dressed like a woman.

Sissy maids were also generally straight males who tried to emulate women. They enjoyed a more servile role in the presence of women. Sissy maids would merrily tend to housekeeping duties and tenderly provide boudoir service just like real female maids. These relationships could often be purely platonic, with the sissy maid deriving her pleasure from her loyal servitude.

Both of these types tended to be extremely shy, understanding personalities. They tended to be extremely sympathetic to women. They also would keep their proclivity to wear female clothing a deep dark secret for fear of ridicule.

In both cases, the male worshipped and adored women to the point of doing anything that a girl might desire. They were very sensitive to the needs and wants of female companionship. It was the worshipping and adoring of women that had caught Robin's attention.

Robin wasn't absolutely certain which category Cheryl fell into. Cheryl had seemed to be happy working at the Aterberry hotel like a female maid. Cheryl had been in close proximity for quite a while, yet she had never even attempted to steal a kiss from her. So Robin guessed that Cheryl must not have a sexual interest in her, that most likely she was probably the sissy maid type.

That was fine with Robin. Cheryl had become a good friend but she had no sexual interest in her either. She enjoyed her company but no more than that. She viewed Cheryl like she would view any other woman. Why would she have a sexual interest in a woman? Particularly one dressed in a maid uniform?

Robin always thought of herself to be a fine woman. A woman worthy of so much more than she had. A woman worthy of having the very best.

So Robin realized that there was a certain plus side to the situation. It was a benefit that she didn't want to let go of. Why should she?

Robin summoned her most authoritative voice.

"Daryl, I can't tell you how disappointed I am in you. But I'm willing to forgive you. But first, you need to do something for me."

Daryl smiled. Perhaps things weren't so bad after all!

"*Anything* that you would like."

"Before I say another word to you, I want Cheryl back, just the way she always looks. Right now!"

That was hardly the response that Daryl expected. But looking at Robin, he knew better than to question her. He quickly went to the bedroom to change back into Cheryl.

Chapter 21. Cheryl Returns

Robin had clearly been adamant. She wanted to see Cheryl, not Daryl. So when Cheryl emerged from her bedroom she was back in her maid uniform, with her wig on, fully made up. Robin smiled when she saw her.

"That's much better. Now we can talk."

Robin was seated on the sofa. Cheryl approached in order to sit down next to her. Robin held up her hand.

"Did I say that you could sit down?"

Cheryl stopped a few steps in front of her. Clearly their relationship had changed. Cheryl stood, hands folded in front of her, eyes lowered submissively. She looked like a little girl about to be chastised by her superior. She felt that way too. Robin continued.

"I trusted you Cheryl. I should throw you out for being so devious. But because I like you I'm willing to forgive you. But I'll only forgive you if you agree to my terms."

Robin paused for emphasis. Cheryl didn't dare say a word. Instead she waited for the verdict.

"Do you think that you were clever by deceiving me? I think not. You played a part that I think deep down you really desire. You may have deceived me, but you didn't deceive yourself.

You wanted to be a girl, so Cheryl, if you are going to stay here, then for your punishment you *will* be a girl. Cheryl is a submissive little obedient girl and you *are* Cheryl. So you will live like a girl and you will act like a girl. I don't *ever* want to see Daryl again. If I ever see any semblance of Daryl again I will throw you out. Do you understand me?"

Cheryl hadn't really wanted to be a girl, but she wasn't about to argue. She had been acting like a girl for months so it didn't seem to be too much to ask of her. She would still be close to Robin so she was really getting exactly what she wanted. So she just nodded her head in agreement. That only irritated Robin that much more.

"Oh, nothing to say for yourself now? I should think that *Yes Miss Robin* would be in order."

Cheryl meekly replied.

"Yes Miss Robin."

"That's better. Much better. You are dressed like a maid. I didn't tell you to dress that way, but that was the outfit you selected to present yourself in. So a maid you shall be. You will be *my* maid and you will do *all* of the jobs that a hired maid would normally do for me. Do you understand me?"

"Yes Miss Robin."

"Very good. Apparently you really *are* a fast learner. I like that in a maid."

Cheryl blushed. She hadn't thought of herself to be *Robin's* maid until that moment. Robin wasn't finished just yet.

"There are dishes to be cleaned in the kitchen. Snap to it girl!"

"Yes Miss Robin."

Just like that Cheryl was off to the kitchen. Robin smiled to herself.

She had never before thought that she could boss a male around like that. But Cheryl had obeyed her without question. Was Cheryl simply that much of a sissy girl? Or was she really that powerful? She was amused by the possibility.

Robin liked her newfound authority. She was moving up in the world. She decided that she could have plenty of fun being in charge like that.

Chapter 22. Relationships

From that point on, the relationship between Robin and Cheryl changed. When Robin saw how Cheryl had reacted to being told that she was a maid, for the first time ever she felt superior to a male. It was a feeling that she liked.

When she pushed Cheryl a bit further, her new maid meekly complied. Initially, it was little things. She had Cheryl bring her a drink while she relaxed. Cheryl made snacks for her. Robin liked the rush of ordering her maid all about.

Then Robin became even more daring. She sent her maid to the hair salon to have her real hair dyed blonde and to get a perm. No more wig for Robin's maid! It left Cheryl with a natural looking curly hairstyle that was distinctly feminine.

Encouraged by those results, Robin had Cheryl get her ears pierced. Since Robin wasn't wearing her jewelry anymore, she gave it all to Cheryl. Then Robin insisted that Cheryl wear earrings, a bracelet, and a necklace every day.

Robin even had Cheryl move her old clothes into Cheryl's closet. Since Robin was no longer wearing cute dresses and skirts, she gave them all to Cheryl.

Women who experience their feminine superiority over a sissy maid seldom want to give up that wonderful feeling. Robin was no different in that regard. She enjoyed toying with Cheryl and watching how the sissy responded to her orders.

The more Robin experienced the thrill of domination, the more she enjoyed it. She decided that she didn't want to ever give up the empowering feeling. Then the answer hit her.

Cheryl wanted to marry her, so why not make the arrangement permanent? Why not marry Cheryl?

Robin smiled at the thought. It would be the perfect way to make certain that Cheryl would remain her maid indefinitely. How delicious!

Robin's proposal was unique. While Robin sat comfortably on the sofa, she had Cheryl kneel down in front of her. Then she presented the ring that she had bought for the occasion.

"Cheryl, I would like you to become my bride. Would you agree to marry me?"

Cheryl couldn't believe what she was hearing. Of course she wanted to marry Robin! She gleefully took the ring and placed it on her finger.

Robin smiled.

"You do realize that I want you to become my *bride*. You will be living with me in the permanent role of my housewife. I do have other conditions. Under no circumstances will I ever allow you to violate me with your…"

She stopped there, searching for words. She wanted to sound firm but not too vulgar. Certain words shouldn't be said aloud! She had to make sure that Cheryl understood.

"…with your *thing*. I'll have none of *that*!"

Cheryl was so excited to marry Robin that perhaps she didn't quite understand the implication.

"That's fine with me. I'll do anything for you."

Chapter 23. Not At All Kinky

Robin didn't want a big to-do of a wedding. No, just a Justice of the Peace and a couple of witnesses would be fine. But she did want to prepare Cheryl for her life of servitude.

She really had no further ideas. After all, Robin wasn't a very uninhibited girl. No, not at all. Mostly, she had just been overcome by the circumstances. That feeling of empowerment was new for her. She had just allowed the feeling to drive her actions.

No, she was not at *all* kinky. Or at least so she thought. Her two sisters, Kendra and Wilma were the kinky ones. Kendra was the oldest, and Wilma was the youngest. They were both well versed in kinky sexual practices. They had often made Robin blush with details of their dates when they were growing up. That gave Robin an idea. She needed witnesses for the wedding anyway, so why not call home and see if her sisters had any ideas about Cheryl?

Kendra answered the phone. When Robin announced her wedding, Kendra called Wilma over and put the call on speaker. Little did Robin know, her Mother Louise was also in the room and she could hear every word.

"Kendra, I'm getting married."

"Really? Tell us *everything*!"

"You know how you used to tease submissive boys? Well, I found one for my very own. Her name is Cheryl."

Robin could hear shrieks of laughter on the other end of the call.

"A sissy girl! Our sister has finally grown up! We knew that you would come around to our way of thinking. We thought that you always were a tomboy at heart."

Robin still wasn't willing to admit the truth.

"I am not. It just worked out that way."

She could hear more laughter on the other end.

"Tell us about your sissy girl. We want to know more."

"She is a cute little thing. Very submissive. I have her in uniform doing housework for me. She seems to get off on it."

Robin's Mother spoke up.

"You'll never do another day of housework again honey. Good job."

Robin was surprised to hear her Mother's voice.

"Hi Mom! I didn't know you were listening. I called for ideas on how to make Cheryl more…*accommodating*. You know, like Kendra used to do with her boyfriends."

Wilma spoke up.

"She still does!"

There was more laughter before her Mother spoke.

"Honey when is the wedding?"

"Whenever you can get over here I'll arrange it."

"How about we come up next week. Kendra says that she has a great idea for Cheryl."

"That sounds good!"

Chapter 24. Preparations

A week had passed since Robin had announced her wedding. Cheryl was still at work when Kendra, Wilma and Louise arrived at the apartment. There were hugs all around until they all sat together and got down to business.

There was a distinct difference between Robin's family and Robin. While Robin was dressed rather masculine, Kendra, Wilma, and Louise were all dressed differently. Kendra wore a little black leather dress that showed plenty of leg and cleavage. In her stiletto heels she was the vision of a strict Dominatrix.

Robin's little sister Wilma, had a similar dress, but lower heels. She seemed more like a Dominatrix in training. On the other hand, Louise was attired in a rose flowered dress more appropriate for a woman of her age. The vivid contrast among the group was evident solely by the clothes that they wore.

Finally, Robin's Mother Louise took charge.

"Here is what we were thinking dear. Wilma and I will get you ready for the big day. Kendra will take care of Cheryl. How does that sound?"

"Great."

Kendra quipped.

"Can I play with her? Can I do *anything* that I want with her?"

Robin nodded.

"Absolutely. Anything you want."

Kendra grinned.

"Great. I'll give her the full treatment."

Louise continued.

"Does Cheryl already have a dress? We wouldn't want her to miss out on being objectified and paraded about like a willing tart."

The girls laughed. Robin smiled. She had that covered.

"Yes, she does. I have one that she can wear."

Louise smiled. Her daughter had obviously been thinking ahead in her relationship. She wanted to show her approval.

"Well done Robin. I wholeheartedly approve of you taking on both a maid and a wife. I do hope that Cheryl is sufficiently submissive. Maids are inherently submissive so it is an important quality."

Robin nodded her head.

"Cheryl makes an excellent maid."

Louise prodded further.

"Will she perform menial tasks? You know, the ones that you don't want to be bothered with? A maid often needs to get her pretty little hands dirty. Will Cheryl do that?"

"Yes Mom."

"Has she gone down on her hands and knees scrubbing floors?"

"Yes Mom."

"Done the laundry?"

"All the time."

"Dishes?"

"Yes Mom."

"I guess I'm satisfied. She sounds like an acceptable maid."

Robin rolled her eyes. Her Mom always wanted the best for her!

Chapter 25. Cheryl Enters

The ladies continued talking about the wedding plans right up until Cheryl came home from work. Then Robin introduced Cheryl to her family. The ladies all sat comfortably while Cheryl, still in her maid uniform, stood self-consciously in front of them. Finally, Louise spoke up.

"So Robin, this is your Tomgirl? She sure looks the part."

"Mom, that term is *so* outdated!"

Louise wasn't particularly dissuaded.

"Well she is, isn't she?"

Kendra laughed at the uneasy exchange.

"Robin, the girl fooled you once. You don't want to be fooled again, do you? I mean, you did check her to see if she really was a sissy girl, didn't you?"

Robin was caught off-guard. She hadn't even thought of that.

"Why, no, I didn't. I took her word for it."

Kendra looked at Louise for approval, grinned, then look back at Cheryl before she continued.

"We need to check. Just to be certain. Cheryl honey, lift your dress up and lower your panties to that we can all have a good look."

Cheryl was clearly uncomfortable doing such a thing in front of all the ladies. However, she could tell by the look the four ladies gave her that she hardly had a say in the matter. She reluctantly lifted her dress with one hand and then clumsily pulled her own panties down with the other.

Kendra burst into laughter.

"No wonder she's a sissy girl. She's practically a real pre-pubescent girl! Not even a hair on her petite sissy clitty! She could scarcely pleasure a woman with such a tiny little thing."

All four ladies laughed in unison while Cheryl turned a deep shade of red. Most who found themselves in such a humiliating situation would immediately cover themselves up. But Cheryl was intimidated by the attractive woman in the leather outfit. She stayed in position, holding her dress up exhibiting her genitals for the amusement of the ladies. The discussion continued while she stood there totally exposed. Kendra composed herself before she spoke again.

"Robin, you do understand that you'll never be satisfied in the bedroom with such a sissy girl, don't you? I mean, *look* at her!"

Robin wasn't deterred in the least.

"I've had enough mauling for a lifetime. Our relationship is platonic. Cheryl is an excellent housekeeper and quite obedient."

Louise nodded her head.

"I should say, she appears to be extremely submissive too."

Louise had a question.

"Robin, dear, did you ever punish Cheryl for deceiving you? I think that it's best to settle such things before the wedding. Don't you agree? You wouldn't want her being dishonest with you again now, would you?"

Chapter 26. Honesty Assured

Robin hadn't really thought about it until that moment. Her Mom was right. Robin wasn't about to let the deception go unpunished. Cheryl would have to be disciplined for attempting to deceive Robin. It was the only way that Robin could think of to assert herself permanently over her bride to be.

"No Mom, I didn't…"

Louise smiled.

"Then we'll have to settle that right now."

Louise reached for her purse and took out a small wooden hairbrush. Then she stood up and moved over to the wooden chair that was by the work desk. She sat down and made herself comfortable. Then she arranged her dress so that it was slightly above her knees, and she smoothed it out. She certainly didn't want her dress to get wrinkled. Then she looked straight at Cheryl.

"Over my knees right this instant girl!"

Cheryl stepped closer to Louise. Much to the surprise of the ladies, Cheryl immediately became fully erect. Though her sissy clit was small, they couldn't help but notice the change. Kendra pointed it out.

"Look at that! The sissy is *turned on* by the thought of a spanking! Talk about submissive!"

The ladies laughed some more at Cheryl's erect condition.

Cheryl quickly realized that she was unable to control her excitement. Much to the amusement of the ladies, Cheryl found herself immediately obeying Louise. She positioned herself over Louise's knees, with her bare bottom in the perfect spanking position. Kendra snickered at the quick response.

"Robin, you're right. She's very obedient. Quite submissive, she'll make a good bride."

Louise smiled at her success in ordering the Tomgirl over her knees.

"Cheryl, you have to promise to obey Robin like a good wife. Agreed?"

There was a meek little response.

"Yes Ma'am."

With that, the hairbrush landed firmly on Cheryl's upturned bottom. Louise continued to lecture while she skillfully applied the hairbrush twenty times in all. Cheryl had to agree to be a faithful wife, to do all of the household chores, and to submit to whatever discipline Robin cared to administer. Each promise was punctuated with the whack of the hairbrush. Cheryl's bottom was a deep red when Louise finished with her. Clearly Louise had experience with discipline sessions.

"If I hear any different, I'll be back here and you'll be over my knees again! Now then, keep holding that dress up and off to the corner with you."

The ladies giggled while Cheryl struggled to get into the corner holding her dress up with her panties still down at her knees. Cheryl remained there while the ladies continued making wedding plans.

Cheryl stayed in the corner, panties down, dress up, until the ladies returned to their hotel room for the night. It was only then that Robin told her that she could go to bed.

Chapter 27. Left Alone

The next morning, Kendra was left with Cheryl to prepare her for the wedding while Robin, Wilma, and Louise went shopping. Kendra had been looking forward to being left alone with Cheryl so that she could check her out for herself. She wanted to tease her and to have a bit of fun with her. They sat next to each other on Cheryl's bed.

"So Cheryl, did you enjoy your little charade? It takes quite a bit of work to pull off a ruse like you did. Imagine pretending to be a girl all that time. My sister fell for you, so I must say, well done!"

Cheryl smiled.

"It was easy really. Once I got the wardrobe down right, the rest just happened."

Kendra disagreed.

"Becoming a woman is more than just putting on the right clothes. There are societal expectations. I'm sure that you've felt them. Guys think that we're just sex objects. We have to work hard to overcome that."

Cheryl told a little lie.

"I hadn't really noticed…"

"You will. A pretty girl like you will always draw attention. There are expectations, even from a married woman. You don't know what it means to be a real woman until you have submitted to a man. Most girls have tasted cock. It is disgusting, but a necessary rite of passage for a girl like you."

Cheryl made a face.

"I could never do that."

"You'll be amazed at what you will do once you are in character. Submission is in your nature. I can tell. That maid uniform you are wearing says it all."

Cheryl didn't believe a word of it. Kendra continued.

"Cheryl dear, most guys think that sex is all about satisfying their cock. But that's not true at all. Sex is about making a woman feel beautiful and most importantly, about giving her pleasure. Don't you agree?"

Cheryl was so taken by the beautiful woman that all she could do was nod her head in agreement.

"You *have* satisfied my sister, haven't you? Not with that *thing* between your legs, but I mean properly. For her pleasure, not for yours. With your tongue. Right?"

Kendra waited for an answer, but Cheryl wasn't sure what to say. In fact, she hadn't even suitably kissed Robin, let alone quenched her sexual cravings. Kendra could tell.

"Holy shit! You haven't *satisfied* her, have you? You're a *fucking* oral *virgin*!"

Kendra made it sound like it was such a terrible thing that had to be rectified immediately. Cheryl looked down at her lap where her hands were folded. She had no idea how she could possibly respond. Kendra knew that she had to fix things for her sister. Besides, it would be fun to teach such a submissive sissy girl the ropes.

"Don't worry sweetie, I'll teach you everything that you need to know."

Kendra repositioned herself on the bed so that she was more comfortable. She took on the manner of a school teacher instructing a little boy how to behave in class.

"Gently take my jeans down. That's right. Now my panties."

Cheryl carefully obeyed. Her eyes widened the first time that she saw Kendra's sex on display. Kendra wasn't at all embarrassed. It was hardly the first time that she had taught a submissive sissy girl how to pleasure her.

She was certain it wouldn't be her last.

Chapter 28. Gifts

By the time the ladies returned from their shopping trip, Kendra had taught Cheryl how to exquisitely pleasure a woman with oral servitude. Kendra had orgasmed twice along the way. Cheryl's face was covered with fragrant feminine musk though she didn't realize it.

Louise announced that it was time for wedding gifts. They all gathered together, with Robin on the sofa in the middle, and with Cheryl standing off to the side.

The most interesting gift Robin opened was a package that contained a double dildo, a strap-on with a large dildo, and a jar of lubricant. The ladies laughed hysterically while Cheryl turned a deep dark shade of red.

Finally it was Cheryl's turn. She had several gifts that were mostly items for the kitchen. Then she opened up a box that was a gift from Wilma. It contained a rhinestone necklace with the word *Slave* written out in the shiny jewels. There was also a matching ankle bracelet with an identification tag that said *Slut*. Wilma helped Cheryl put them both on. The necklace fit perfectly. It was tight against Cheryl's neck with the word Slave prominently displayed in front. The ankle bracelet punctuated the message.

Cheryl squirmed uncomfortably while the ladies clapped their approval. They all agreed that it was perfect for the wedding day and that surely Robin would have the jewelry adorn Cheryl every day after that.

Cheryl's last package, however, contained a faux silicon prosthetic vagina. While the ladies giggled, Kendra spoke up.

"With that tiny little clit you have, once you put that on you'll look and feel like a *real* lady! I'm sure that Robin will want you to wear it all the time. Let's go try it on!"

Kendra took Cheryl by the hand and led her back to her bedroom. While Kendra worked with Cheryl, the other ladies stayed talking about the wedding day. Everything was set. There would be a quick ceremony at the Justice of the Peace followed by a dinner at a local restaurant. Louise had reserved a private room for the occasion. Louise had also arranged for a white limo to chauffeur everybody around.

Finally Kendra emerged from the bedroom leading Cheryl by her hand. She brought Cheryl in front of the group and then told her to lift her dress so that everybody could see how she looked.

Cheryl was fast becoming accustomed to doing what she was told to do. Without hesitation, she lifted her dress to show off her new present.

Kendra had put Cheryl in a frilly pair of panties and garter with stockings over her faux vagina. The prosthesis went on like a pair of panties and fit her like a second skin. It not only hid her male parts, it plumped up her bottom. The ladies smiled their approval. Kendra gave them the highlights.

"See how smooth she looks? She's anatomically correct! Very authentic. Her clitty is secured in a sheath that will keep it out of the way. It will still allow her to pee while sitting down. Take those panties down girl and show us."

Cheryl timidly lowered her panties. The ladies smiled their approval at her realistic vagina before Kendra continued.

"Turn around Cheryl."

The sissy obeyed.

"There are front and back openings for full penetration. I'm sure that Robin will take full advantage!"

Again the ladies laughed. They had never had so much fun!

Cheryl felt that the vagina gave her a feminine feeling to go along with her new feminine image. Her sissy clitty was snug inside the sheath. She now had a presentation in front just like a woman. Tucked in the way it was, she knew that she would be unable to achieve an erection. All of the stretchy material would see to that. But that didn't bother her at all.

After all, real maids don't get hard-ons!

Chapter 29. Wedding Bells

Kendra, Wilma, and Louise arrived early on the morning of the wedding. Kendra had Cheryl put on a nylon blouse and a mini skirt so that they could go to the salon to have her hair and makeup done. While they were gone, Louise and Wilma were to get Robin ready for her big day.

Cheryl had only been to a salon on a couple of occasions to have her hair done so she was still anxious about being there. Kendra made sure that all of the employees knew that Cheryl was getting married. The stylist, June, and the makeup artist, Emily, both did a good job of putting her at ease.

To Cheryl, it seemed like she was at the salon for days. While June fussed over her hair, another young lady did her nails. They both finished at about the same time. June added a final blast of hairspray while Cheryl put her hands under the drying lamp.

Once the stylist finished with her hair, the makeup artist went to work. She started with lash extensions, then moved on to airbrushing a foundation. Cheryl was becoming impatient with the whole process while Emily continued fussing over her eyes. Emily assured her that it would all be worth the time she spent making her into the absolute perfect bride.

The ladies didn't allow Cheryl to look in the mirror until they had finished with their magic. When they finally showed Cheryl how she looked, she could hardly believe it. She didn't even recognize herself!

Her hair looked like it was out of a storybook. Her blonde hairdo was topped with a flower headpiece that made her look like a princess. She had smokey bedroom eyes. Each blink of her long lashes beckoned a suitor to woo her into bed.

Cheryl had never had her foundation airbrushed so perfectly before. Her skin looked flawless. With her rosy cheeks, she appeared to be innocently blushing with ardent anticipation. Her glossy wet lips longed to be kissed.

Kendra was certainly pleased. She paid the ladies with a generous tip and led Cheryl back to the apartment to get her dressed for the wedding.

When they arrived at the apartment, Cheryl could hear the other ladies talking in Robin's bedroom. The door was closed so she couldn't see what they were doing, but they were giggling so she thought that they must be having a good time.

When Kendra led Cheryl into her own bedroom, it hit Cheryl what was really going to happen. Robin's wedding dress was arranged neatly on the bed just waiting for Cheryl to slip into it.

Cheryl began to protest, but Kendra put a quick stop to it.

"Now, now, all brides are nervous on their wedding day. Let's just get you into your dress and I'm sure you'll feel just fine."

"But, but…"

Kendra held up the white dress for Cheryl to see.

"Shush honey. Trust me, you'll look amazing in this. Let me help you. Strip down. Take it all off, including undies."

For Cheryl it was all a blur. She stripped down to her fake vagina without a fuss. Kendra had lingerie ready too. In moments, Cheryl was in a white lace push-up bra that Kendra said flattered her breasts. A lace garter belt with white stockings followed before she stepped into matching white lace panties. Kendra added a lace bridal garter that she adjusted for Cheryl.

Kendra heavily misted Cheryl with a fragrant perfume.

By the time Kendra put Cheryl in a full slip, zipped Cheryl into her wedding gown and had her slip on her white heels, there was no mistaking what Cheryl had become. Adorned with her rhinestone *Slave* necklace, matching earrings, and slut ankle bracelet, she was the picture of a blushing bride on her wedding day. She could not possibly be mistaken for anything other than a young lady on her way to a wedding. Her obvious shyness coupled with her flushed embarrassment at being dressed like a female bride only added to her authentic look. Most brides feel that way on their wedding day!

Finally it was time to go. Kendra handed Cheryl a bouquet of flowers. The chauffeur was at the door, and Cheryl could hear the ladies talking just outside her room.

When Kendra led Cheryl out of her bedroom, she was surprised at what she saw. Robin was dressed in a white tuxedo, complete with cummerbund, looking very much like a dashing young man on his way to his wedding.

While Wilma took several pictures of the couple with her cell, the chauffeur gazed at Cheryl with hungry eyes. Cheryl realized that she wouldn't have to worry about not passing for a girl on this day. She may as well just relax. No problem at all!

When they arrived at the Justice of the Peace, everyone stopped to watch the bride and groom. Cheryl could feel their eyes all over her. It was very discomforting for her. In no time at all they were ready for the ceremony.

Chapter 30. Vows

"Do you take this woman to be your lawfully wedded wife, to have and to hold for as long as you wish?"

Robin smiled.

"I do."

"Do you take this man to be your lawfully wedded husband, to love, honor, and obey?"

Cheryl blushed even more than she had been blushing all day.

"I do."

"I now pronounce you husband and wife."

He turned to Robin.

"You may now kiss the bride."

It was the first real kiss that Cheryl had with Robin. She closed her eyes and relished the deep kiss that Robin gave her. Their tongues danced together in ardent hunger. Cheryl had actually married Robin, even if it was under rather strange circumstances.

The Justice of the Peace looked at Kendra, Wilma, and Louise.

"I now present Mr. and Mrs. Robin Dearing."

Cheryl broke out of her fog for just a second. *Dearing*? Her name was now Cheryl *Dearing*?

She opened her mouth to comment but Robin smothered her with another deep kiss before she could say a word.

Then it was on to the reception.

At the restaurant strangers came to their table to offer congratulations. Cheryl had never before felt so sexually objectified. Women looked at her necklace with disapproval. Guys who came by chuckled at her obvious submissive nature and then leered at her.

The gaudy necklace made Cheryl feel self-conscious but she didn't dare remove it. Instead, she smiled at all of the comments and sat like a good girl with the rest of the ladies.

Chapter 31. Bridal Suite

The chauffeur dropped Robin and Cheryl off at their apartment. It was only there, in the silence of the bedroom that Cheryl began to think about what the night might bring. Robin didn't waste any time.

She quickly unzipped Cheryl's dress and stripped her down to her underwear. Then she took Cheryl and led her into her bedroom where she had her bride lay face down on the bed. Cheryl's panties came off before Robin spread her legs wide.

Cheryl knew what was going to happen before she felt the lubricant being worked into her rear. She didn't want to be penetrated like that but she wanted Robin to have what *she* wanted.

She changed her mind when she felt the large dildo up against her anal opening. She was about to protest when Robin leaned into her and shoved the dildo right up her ass. Cheryl let out a gasp that Robin took to be excitement.

Robin proceeded to take out all of the frustration she had built up with guys over the years. She pumped Cheryl like she was a willingly paid whore. Cheryl quickly found the forced prostrate massage to be rather pleasant so she stopped struggling. Somewhere in the excitement Robin had an amazing orgasm from the double dildo that she had been putting to good use on Cheryl's bottom.

Robin was so aroused that one orgasm wasn't enough. She took off the dildo and positioned herself on her back. She gave Cheryl a stern look.

"Pleasure me."

Cheryl tenderly pulled Robin's pants and panties off. Then she buried her face in Robin's pussy just the way Kendra had taught her to do. Then she toyed with Robin's clitoris with the tip of her tongue until she drove Robin wild with lust. Finally in a spurt of feminine moisture, Robin had the orgasm of a lifetime, her second of the night.

Robin fell into a deep sleep while Cheryl stayed next to her staring up at the ceiling. She was aroused but fully frustrated from the experience.

Cheryl took consolation in that she had married Robin and that Robin had, in a way, consummated their marriage in the bedroom. Still, staring up at the ceiling in the dark, she couldn't help but think about the terms that Robin had dictated to her.

She was to be a traditional wife, more housemaid than equal partner. She had agreed to be obedient to Robin's every whim. Plus, with Robin in disguise appearing to be male, Cheryl had committed to keeping her appearance female. She even had Robin's last name to prove it.

Now she was legally Cheryl *Dearing*!

Chapter 32. The Morning After

The next morning Cheryl was out of bed first. She silently tip-toed back to her own bedroom to change her clothes and to freshen up. She was surprised when she saw herself in the mirror that morning.

She looked very much like a woman who had frolicked in the bedroom all night long. The flowers that had been in her were gone. Her hair was mussed and her lipstick was smeared all over her face. While she cleaned herself up she reminded herself to always check her makeup after satisfying Robin. Kendra had left that part out.

After she changed into a housedress, Cheryl went to the kitchen to start breakfast. Robin appeared a few minutes later looking radiant, like she always did. After they ate breakfast, Robin slowly sipped a cup of coffee while they talked.

"Well Cheryl, you performed very nicely last night. I do want to remind you of our arrangement."

Robin had Cheryl's full attention while she continued.

"I am in charge in this household and you are not to take sexual liberties. I want you wearing your necklace, ankle bracelet, and your fake vagina at all times. Just to be clear, I mean *both* inside and outside the apartment. That way there will be no misunderstandings. I have no intention of ever letting you pleasure yourself inside of me."

Cheryl had hoped that she could take the necklace off after the wedding but it seemed that Robin was insistent that she wear it. She would have to make due. She had already accepted that Robin wouldn't allow her to have conventional sex. That was understood. Robin continued.

"You'll have to continue working at The Aterberry so that we can pay all the bills. When you are at home I want you to stay in your maid uniform and tend to household chores and to my needs.

Oh, and I don't know how you learned to pleasure with your tongue like you did last night, but you can count on doing that often. Do you get the picture?"

"Yes Ma'am."

Cheryl understood completely.

Chapter 33. Back To Work

The newlyweds didn't really have a honeymoon—they simply couldn't afford to go anywhere. So just a couple of days after the wedding Robin returned to her job and Cheryl had to go back to work too. When they handed out cleaning assignments at the hotel, Cheryl's supervisor told her that her relatives were staying on the third floor—so Cheryl was re-assigned to clean that floor.

All of the ladies at the hotel assumed that Cheryl had a traditional marriage. They thought that Robin was a guy and that Cheryl was a girl. They had no reason to think otherwise.

The other maids had teased Cheryl when they saw her necklace. They laughed when they said that she would make a good sexual slave and that she should be careful not to get herself pregnant too soon. They wanted to know all of the details about the wedding, and of course, the wedding night. Cheryl managed to change enough details so that they had no idea what had actually happened.

The younger maids giggled at her description of her lover. They wanted to know how big Robin's cock was and if she had any trouble accepting it. They also asked how many times did he spurt into her and did she orgasm too?

The older maids warned her that she should take good care of Robin because guys often leave their wives. They emphasized that a woman's place is to please her husband and that Cheryl shouldn't ever forget it.

For Cheryl it was quite amusing considering her actual situation. She just laughed it all off. It felt good to be back on the job.

She hadn't worked on the third floor before, so it was a nice diversion from her usual routine. When she opened the door to the suite where her in-laws were staying, she was surprised to find that they hadn't left for home yet.

She immediately offered to come back later, but Louise insisted that they didn't mind if she started to clean their suite while they were still in the room.

Kendra couldn't help herself.

"You look well fucked this morning. Did Robin screw you like a French whore?"

Cheryl blushed. Kendra immediately knew the truth. She didn't need to hear an answer.

"She fucked you good! I knew it."

Louise interrupted.

"Kendra, can't you see she's shy. Leave her alone. I'm sure that Robin was well satisfied. I'm sure that Cheryl took good care of her. Let's leave the maid alone and go to breakfast."

Wilma was still getting dressed in the bathroom. She called out.

"You two go ahead. I'll catch up later."

Louise and Kendra went out the door while Cheryl started stripping the bed. She had just finished putting new sheets on when Wilma came out of the bathroom. She was wearing a white blouse and a red miniskirt.

Wilma moved in front of Cheryl and sat down on the bed. Then she crossed her legs. She whispered seductively while she smoothed her stockings, drawing Cheryl's attention to her legs.

"Cheryl, do you like what you see?"

Chapter 34. Seduction

Cheryl couldn't help but stare at Wilma's attractive legs. Sitting the way Wilma was, her red miniskirt showed just about everything all the way up to her panties. She nodded her head in muted approval of Wilma's lovely vision.

Wilma changed her tone, now speaking in a flirtatious manner.

"Kendra tells me that you think that girls are superior to boys. Is that true?"

Cheryl's throat was dry, but she still managed to answer.

"Yes…Ma'am."

She thought that adding Ma'am would help keep things professional. Instead, the deference served to encourage Wilma.

"That must be why you prefer to be a girl. You do make a very pretty girl. Have you ever worn a sweater dress? I'll bet a sweater dress would really bring out your breasts."

Wilma continued to stroke her legs. Her hands went all the way down to her ankles and then up to the top of her thighs. Cheryl's eyes stayed riveted on the pantyhose tease.

Cheryl didn't answer her question. It had been months since she had been sexually satisfied. She had never experienced such sexual frustration before in her life. Her mind was off in another world, fantasizing about the beauty who was tempting her that very moment. Wilma continued to tease her.

"Kendra told me that you are quite an expert with your tongue. She said that you really knew how to pleasure a woman. Is that true?"

With those last words, Wilma slid her skirt up. Cheryl could see that she had no panties on under her pantyhose. She could see that Wilma's pubes were shaved clean. The vision of womanhood was almost too much for the sissy maid.

"Wilma, I'm a married woman…"

Her voice trailed off while Wilma slid her pantyhose down. Then she used her most seductive voice.

"Would you like to pleasure me sweetie?"

That was all that Cheryl could take. She immediately dropped to her knees in front of Wilma and buried her tongue deep inside of the seductress. Then she withdrew and softly teased her precious vaginal lips with tiny little licks. Wilma laughed at how easy it had been to dominate the sissy girl while the maid willingly lapped away like a slutty slave girl.

When Cheryl's tongue found Wilma's clit, the young girl moaned in ecstasy. She had wanted to enjoy Cheryl's delights since that first day that she saw her and her dream was coming true. She wrapped her legs around the maid holding her in place while her sexual needs were serviced.

Cheryl didn't know what came over her. She couldn't help herself. She teased Wilma with her tongue every way that Kendra had taught her. Her sister-in-law writhed in pleasure while Cheryl bathed her own face with Wilma's feminine musk.

Cheryl had her tongue deep inside Wilma's vagina when Wilma began to arch her hips upward. Cheryl slowed down her tongue worship in order to maximize Wilma's pleasure.

Wilma's nipples needed attention but she dared not divert Cheryl from her ministrations. Wilma moved her own hands underneath her blouse, under her bra, and to her own taut nipples. She fondled them herself, increasing the intensity of the pleasure that she was relishing.

The glow deep inside of Wilma became a raging fire. Her muscles twitched in wanton anticipation. Her hands joined her legs holding Cheryl in place. Her juices were flowing freely until, in a final burst of ultimate pleasure, Wilma let out an orgasmic scream. Pleasure rippled through her body from top to bottom while she humped Cheryl's tongue like a French whore.

Wilma collapsed in exhaustion. Cheryl, still highly aroused, thought that she had best leave her sister-in-law before she lost control of herself. She quickly went into the bathroom and fixed her lipstick. Her face was pleasantly perfumed with Wilma's musk. It was intoxicating. She decided not to wash her face.

Cheryl stepped out into the hall to catch her breath. She hadn't finished the room, but she could come back later. She quickly rolled her cleaning cart on to the next room so she could continue her work.

Chapter 35. Third Floor Trevor

Cheryl didn't realize who else was on the third floor until she was on her fifth room of the day. She completed making the bed when the bathroom door opened. She hadn't realized that there was anybody else in the room. She was shocked to find Robin's old boyfriend Trevor leering at her.

Of course Trevor hadn't met Cheryl before so he had no idea who she was. Cheryl only knew Trevor because Robin had shown her a cell phone photo. She immediately knew that she had to find a way out of the room. Trevor spoke first.

"My, my, who do we have here? Such a pretty young maid."

He took a few steps towards her. He could smell the familiar feminine scent of excitement on the maid. Though it was actually Wilma's musk he was inhaling, he mistook the fragrance for the maid's scent. He reasoned that she was excited by him, and that she wanted him to take her.

Cheryl could see the lust in his eyes. She backed up while he continued.

"I like your necklace sweetie pie. It says a lot about you."

Cheryl took another step back.

"It was a gift…"

He smiled at his good luck. So many women don't want to admit their sexual preference. He had taken so many of them that he had come to realize that they all just needed encouragement. This blonde bimbo would be easy prey for him.

"Sexual submission is nothing to be ashamed of. I didn't need to see your necklace to know the truth about you. Don't be scared honey. I think you'll enjoy what I have in mind for you."

But she *was* scared. She continued moving backwards until she was up against the bed. Then he lunged forward at her and pushed her onto the bed, immediately pinning her down on her back.

"I'm going to fuck your brains out dear. At least what little brains you might have."

He held her hands up over her head while his mouth found hers. She did her best to struggle but he was simply too strong for her to fight him off. She remembered that Robin had said that she had kicked him in the groin to repel his advances. But it was too late. He had already pulled her pantyhose down to her knees so she was helplessly restrained by her own hosiery.

He continued to smother her with deep kisses while she frantically struggled. The weight of his body slowly wore her down until she was unable to mount any more than a feeble defense. The combination of a useless tussle and a longing for sexual relief was too much for the maid to fend off. When he slid her pantyhose off and lifted her dress up, all she could do was whimper a meek little "no." That was all she was able to say before he covered her mouth again with his.

He probed her mouth at will. She began to writhe with pleasure. She pressed her hips to his. She found being mauled by a guy to be repulsive, but she had no willpower left. She stopped fighting him and completely surrendered.

Apparently her faux vagina was good enough to fool him. With one thrust he shoved his cock deep inside and he began to have his way with her. With her balls tucked and her penis safely in its sheath, she could feel his lust pounding against her pubic bone.

It had been so long since Cheryl had an orgasm that being raped actually excited her. When she moaned in ecstasy it only served to encourage him. He sped up the tempo and she continued to raise her hips in rhythm to meet him. Trevor made no effort to slow down or to pleasure her. Instead he fucked her like a chimpanzee conquering a female out in the wild.

Cheryl had heard about women faking orgasms. The other maids had talked regularly about how they fooled their boyfriends and husbands. That was how they put off advances that they were no longer interested in. But none of the ladies ever discussed the frustration of tending to a male and not to their own needs.

Cheryl learned first-hand how that felt when Trevor stiffened and pumped her faux vagina full of his sticky lust. She could feel his rod pulsating and spurting semen even through her silicone love nest. When he was finally spent, he immediately stopped kissing her and momentarily pressed his full weight on to her while he regained his composure.

The indirect contact caused Cheryl to get close to an orgasm, but she fell short. Instead, she had been used by him like a sex object to give him gratification, but she had received none of her own. Much to her dismay, she was disheveled and completely frustrated.

While he stood up and straightened himself out, Cheryl

remembered what Kendra had told her. "Most guys think that sex is all about satisfying their cock."

That was precisely what Trevor had accomplished. Trevor certainly showed no remorse for what he had done. He had pumped her vagina full of semen and just like that he was ready to move on. He helped her off the bed and took her immediately to the door before pushing her out into the hallway.

She stood outside his room and tried to tidy herself up. He had kept her panties for a souvenir of his conquest so she had none to wear. She smoothed her dress and straightened her apron. She would need to freshen her lipstick again as soon as she could find a mirror. Standing without her pantyhose on, she felt cheap and used. She decided not to say anything about the encounter to anyone. The less said about the tawdry affair the better.

She moved on to the next room. She wondered how many other maids had been taken advantage of by the same lowlife in a similar manner. She tried not to think about it.

Chapter 36. Suspended

The next morning, when Cheryl arrived at work, Hilda, who was still her supervisor, called her into her office.

"I have a complaint from Mr. Tolworth on the third floor. He said that you made advances towards him and that you tried to tear his clothes off. He said he tried to fend you off but it was no good. He even produced a pair of his underpants that were torn to prove it. I can't say how disappointed I am in you Cheryl. A married woman behaving like that! Have you no shame? What have you to say for yourself?"

Cheryl hardly knew what to say. Of course none of that was true, it was all a fabrication. He had raped *her*! But apparently Hilda believed Trevor. It was easier to deal with Cheryl than it was to try and learn the truth.

"That's not what happened…"

"Am I to believe you, a mere maid? Mr. Tolworth is a pillar of the community. He has just reserved the entire third floor of The Aterberry for the exclusive use of his company while his company is in transition. How dare you question his account! You are just a maid, and not a very good one at that! I've no doubt that you threw yourself at him in a fit of lust!"

"But…but…"

"Cheryl, you should be fired for such insolence. But it is difficult to find help, and, I might add, quite a bother. So just this once I'm going to be lenient. You are suspended for two weeks without pay. Go home and meditate on your behavior. When you come back I should expect your libido to be under better control."

Cheryl couldn't believe it. Not only was his story completely fictitious, she was going to have her pay docked. Robin needed her paycheck to pay the rent. Two weeks off would make it impossible to pay the month's rent.

When Cheryl arrived back at the apartment, Robin still had not left for the day. Cheryl explained that she had been suspended, but she just said for disciplinary reasons. She left out the part about Trevor. Robin was angry with her. She told her that she would have to find another job in a hurry or they would be behind in their apartment rent.

Robin went out the door to work, leaving Cheryl to sit in disbelief over what had happened. She was brooding over her situation when there was a knock at the door. When she opened the door, she was surprised to see her Mother-in-law Louise with Kendra and Wilma. She invited them in.

Louise went straight to the point.

"I received a call this morning from my daughter. She told me that you have been suspended from your job. Not only that, but Wilma told me that you seduced her. Is that also true?"

Cheryl didn't know what to say. Yes she *had* been suspended. But she didn't dare call Wilma a liar. She didn't want to admit to seducing Wilma either. Robin would surely find out if she admitted to that. She stood silent while she decided what she should do. Louise didn't wait too long.

"I take by your silence that you are guilty on both accounts. I must say that I am greatly disappointed in you Cheryl. You haven't even been married a week and you are already cheating on your husband—and a Lesbian affair to boot!"

Cheryl noticed that her Mother-in-law was carrying a large purse. She immediately found out why. Louise pulled out a large wooden paddle from her purse and glared at Cheryl. The woman obviously meant business.

Cheryl finally found her voice.

"No, please, I can explain. Please don't…"

Louise took her by the hand and led her over to the same wooden chair that she had sat at the last time Cheryl was spanked. Cheryl's first thought was that her fake silicone vagina would at least help to lessen the pain this time. She was wrong about that.

Louise took the sissy over her lap and raised her dress. She yanked Cheryl's panties down and began to lecture her.

"You didn't even last a week before you cheated on my daughter!"

Whack! The wooden paddle made a loud noise when it struck the bottom that was firmly encased in tight silicone. Much to Cheryl's dismay, the silicone prison plumped her bottom up so the spanking was even *more* painful than before. Plus, in her front, her sex was encased in a silicone sleeve that kept it positioned out of the way and unable to become erect.

The sting of the paddle seemed to go straight thru her right to the base of her fake vagina. The ripple of vibration caused a stirring that was not to be satisfied.

"Don't you dare cheat on my daughter again!"

Whack! This time Louise paddled even harder. She was just

warming up!

Whack! Whack! Whack!

The spanking continued. Cheryl thought that she heard somebody else come into the room.

Whack! Whack! Whack!

Louise showed no mercy to the sissy girl. Cheryl squirmed and wriggled while her Mother-in-law turned her bottom a stinging red underneath the silicon. Then the spanking stopped.

"I think you've had enough dear."

Cheryl was relieved. Then she heard a second voice.

"Mother, I don't think she's had enough. She's such a slut, she deserves more!"

Cheryl couldn't believe it. *Wilma* was telling her Mother to spank her even more!

Louise landed another flurry of hits to her upraised bottom. Cheryl could hear Wilma giggling. Finally, Cheryl stopped struggling and surrendered to the inevitable. She lay prone over Louise's lap while her Mother-in-law flailed away mercilessly.

When Louise finished, she sent Cheryl off to the corner. Louise then spoke to Wilma.

"I've got shopping to do with Kendra before we leave. Stay here and make sure she doesn't leave that corner until I get back."

Cheryl heard the click of Louise's heels leaving the room.

Chapter 37. Wilma

Cheryl stayed obediently in the corner with her nose pressed against the wall. Suddenly she heard Wilma whispering in her ear.

"Very good Cheryl. You took that spanking like a naughty little girl. I think that you are very obedient. I like that in a sissy."

Wilma smacked the sissy on her bottom with her open hand.

"You can come out of the corner now. I want to play."

Cheryl responded, still facing the wall.

"Your Mother said not to…"

"Didn't you hear me? I said come out of the corner. Do you want another spanking?"

Cheryl meekly turned around to face Wilma. The young girl shook her head in displeasure.

"Pull your panties up girl, and straighten your dress. You look like a horny tart."

Cheryl immediately complied. Then Wilma took her by the hand.

"Come with me sissy girl. I want to see if you can improve on yesterday's performance."

Wilma led Cheryl into Cheryl's bedroom and then positioned

herself on the bed. She seemed to be annoyed that the sissy maid hadn't quite caught on yet.

"Well, what are you waiting for?"

"But, I…can't…"

"Do I have to get the paddle?"

Cheryl's bottom was already stinging from the spanking that she had just received. Another spanking would be absolutely unbearable.

That morning Wilma had Cheryl give her two blissful orgasms. The sissy girl had obediently complied with every instruction that she gave her. After her second orgasm, Wilma had taken the sissy over her lap and applied the paddle. She feigned that she had not been properly satisfied and she told the sissy that she would have to do better next time.

After that she sent the sissy maid back to the corner with her dress held high and with her panties down at her ankles. There, Cheryl remained until Louise and Kendra returned from their shopping trip.

Wilma realized that what Kendra had taught her about submissive sissy girls was absolutely true. They simply cannot resist the orders of an assertive female. Cheryl was proof of that. She had been unable to resist the authority of Wilma—a girl who was even younger than Cheryl.

Wilma smiled. It had been lots of fun!

Chapter 38. Contrite

Two weeks had gone by and it was time for Cheryl to go back to work. Because of Cheryl's suspension, Robin was a month behind in her rent payment, so Cheryl was desperate to continue working. She reported to Hilda's office, dressed in her maid uniform, all ready to resume her duties. Hilda sat behind her desk and leaned forward to speak with Cheryl.

"I presume that you've learned your lesson girl. But you aren't going to get off that easy. Mr. Tolworth insists on giving you another chance so I'm assigning you full-time to the third floor. Thankfully for you, I believe that he has taken a fancy to you. The first thing you are to do is to go to his suite and give him a proper apology for your outrageous behavior. You must do that in order to resume your employment. Make sure that you are especially contrite dear. I will check with him later to be sure that he is sufficiently satisfied. Do you understand me?"

Cheryl couldn't believe it. *She* had to apologize to *him*! It wasn't fair. It wasn't fair at all. But she desperately needed the job.

"Yes Ma'am."

"You are dismissed."

Cheryl turned to leave. If there was anything that Hilda disliked, it was a snotty maid who showed no respect. She thought that she would teach the girl a lesson about respect.

"Wait!"

Cheryl turned back to face her employer.

"I will not put up with any more nonsense from you. Show your contrition to me girl. Curtsy for me."

Cheryl couldn't believe the woman. She was just trying to add salt to the wound. Regardless, Cheryl managed to dip a dainty little curtsy for her superior.

"Very good girl. I'll make a proper Aterberry maid of you yet. You may go."

With that Cheryl was off to Mr. Tolworth's suite.

Chapter 39. Personal Maid

Cheryl tapped lightly on the door. Mr. Tolworth opened the door and motioned her in. He was wearing a business suit, and a smug look of satisfaction that Cheryl desperately wanted to wipe off his face. He sat down on the edge of the bed while Cheryl stood in front of him, eyes lowered, trying to appear to be apologetic.

"Well girl, do you have something to say to me?"

Cheryl summoned all of the strength that she could muster.

"I'm sorry Mr. Tolworth for what happened before."

He spoke in a superior voice.

"That will hardly do honey. You don't sound at all remorseful. So let me explain the situation to that empty blonde head of yours. We both know that you desperately need this job. I think that you'll do just about *anything* to keep it. Don't get any ideas either. If you leave employment here, I'll make sure that you never work another day in your life. Do you understand what I'm saying?"

Cheryl knew he was right. She had to have the job. Robin was already angry enough at her. If she lost the job it would be a complete disaster. Robin would never forgive her. She summoned her most remorseful voice.

"Yes Mr. Tolworth, I do understand."

"Very good dear. So now you are going to kneel down in front of me and then you will beg me to forgive you. Then you will tell me that you'll do *anything* to please me. Well?"

Cheryl struggled with the urge to tell him where he could go. It was a simple lack of options that caused her to do what she did next. In an act of self-degradation, she lifted her dress slightly above her knees and then she knelt down in front of him. She couldn't look at him. Instead she fixed her eyes at his feet while she spoke.

"Please sir, I'm *so* sorry. I beg you for your forgiveness. I'll do *anything* to satisfy you. Please sir, forgive me."

Cheryl felt like she couldn't possibly have degraded herself any more than that. But Mr. Tolworth was far from satisfied. He continued with the same superior tone.

"I'll do with you what I please. Right now, I'm wondering. Are you wearing panties today? As I recall, you only wore pantyhose when you attempted to rape me. No doubt it was part of your pre-meditated plan. Well?"

Cheryl blushed red.

"Yes, just pantyhose sir."

"Why do I not believe you? You've proven to be somewhat of an untruthful hussy. I understand that you even denied that you tore my clothes off. I need to verify that you are telling me the truth. Lift your dress girl so that I may see for myself."

The nerve! Cheryl couldn't conceive of what was happening to her. She was being treated like a sex object. Didn't he know what she really was? Apparently not!

He was so conceited! She obediently lifted her dress so that the arrogant ass could get a good look at her faux privates right through her pantyhose.

"Don't worry honey. I have something else in mind today."

He undid his belt and then he slid his pants off. He wasn't wearing any underwear either. From where Cheryl was kneeling she had a good look at his genitalia. She was mortified to see that he had a firm erection.

Chapter 40. Slut

Trevor pointed and motioned her towards his cock. Cheryl couldn't have been more repulsed than she was at that moment. But she didn't move away. Instead she tried to protest.

"Please, I can't. I'll never!

"You *can* and you *will*. I can see it in your eyes. You may pleasure me willingly or I can take you over my knee first and then you will pleasure me. But you will submit. It's in your nature. I can tell."

How did he know? It was like he could see right thru her. Cheryl felt a ripple of pleasure and she felt her face flush a deep red. He had threatened to spank her! She hadn't realized the effect such talk had on her. She could only hope that he didn't notice. If he did she wouldn't be able to resist. It was already too late. He grinned hungrily at her.

"You don't fool me girl. I can see the arousal written all over you. What will it be? Surrender or be spanked?"

Cheryl's face burned with lust. The brute! He had her and he knew it. She summoned all of her courage. Then she obediently came forward, lowered her head, and took his full cock into her mouth. Her groaned with lust.

"Very good. I knew you were good for more than just cleaning the room. Slowly. Yes, like that. Touch just the tip. Yes. You're good at this."

Cheryl could hear his breathing change. Now he was

breathing hard and leaning into her face with his hips. She knew what would happen if she continued. But she was afraid to stop. If she did, she knew what would happen. He would raise her dress and lower her pantyhose for her spanking. Then he might find out the truth about her. She couldn't allow that!

Yet she was repulsed by the notion of swallowing his cum. She had no trouble giving oral pleasure to Robin. She didn't even have a problem pleasuring Kendra when she was taught how to pleasure a woman. It hadn't even been that bad serving Wilma. But she had never thought that she would have to give pleasure to a guy.

But there she was. Down on her knees like a common whore, servicing his manhood in the most shameful way possible. She could already taste his precum, and she knew the worst was yet to come.

She thought about the ankle bracelet that Wilma had given her that she was wearing. *Slut*. Kendra had said that she wasn't a real woman until she tasted cum. She had also said how degrading it could be.

Cheryl's thoughts were interrupted with the pulsating of Trevor's cock. Then it erupted in a burst of salty semen that filled her mouth with the disgusting taste.

Trevor held her head firmly in place while she reluctantly swallowed every last drop. She had to. A submissive girl would do the same. Then he made her clean his cock by licking every bit off. Only after that did he finally released her.

Cheryl decided to come back to clean his room later in the day. Perhaps he would be gone by then. When she stepped out the door waves of shame crossed her mind.

What had she done?

Chapter 41. Guilt

Cheryl continued cleaning her other guest rooms with a profound sense of guilt. How could she ever face Robin after what she had done? She shouldn't have given in to Trevor so easily. Yet she hadn't been able to help herself.

Cheryl was walking between rooms, still preoccupied in somewhat of a daze, when Felicity, another maid, passed her by.

"Are you okay Cheryl? You don't look like your usual self. You had better touch up your lipstick and comb your hair before Hilda sees you."

Cheryl went into the next room and took a look at herself in the bathroom mirror. Her lipstick was smeared and her hair was tussled. She looked like the tramp that she felt like.

She quickly fixed her hair and touched up her lipstick before continuing her work. Her mind stayed on Trevor rather than on her work. What had she gotten herself into? How would she deal with Trevor tomorrow? She knew that he would keep coming on to her.

She could still taste his sex in her mouth. It was an awful lingering reminder of what she had done.

When she finished her shift, Hilda approached her in the locker room.

"I have something for you. Trevor said that you gave him an adequate apology and that he is looking forward to seeing you every day. I assured him that you would be assigned permanently to his floor. Well done."

"Thank you Ma'am."

"Oh, and he said to give you this."

She handed Cheryl an envelope. Then Hilda walked away.

Cheryl opened up the envelope. She rolled her eyes in disgust. How could he? Trevor had given her a cash tip for good service. Cheryl couldn't believe it. She felt like a paid whore.

But she could use the cash. She put the envelope in her uniform pocket.

Chapter 42. A Good Look

The next day Cheryl left Trevor's room for last. She was wishing that he would leave before she got there. Her hopes were dashed when she came into the room only to find him waiting for her.

"In the future I expect to be serviced first thing in the morning. I find it best to start the day that way. I have a gift for you."

Cheryl couldn't imagine what sort of gift that Trevor could come up with for her. He pointed to the closet by the doorway. Cheryl tentatively opened the door.

There she found a brand-new maid uniform hanging by itself. She looked at him with a puzzled expression. He encouraged her.

"Try it on. I think you'll like it."

Cheryl pulled the dress out of the closet. At first glance it appeared to be just another maid uniform, typical of the uniforms that all the girls at Aterberry wore. She took a step towards the bathroom so that she could change in private. Trevor immediately objected.

"No, stay here. I want to watch you change."

How dare him! Cheryl wanted to protest, but then she thought about Hilda and about keeping her job. So she decided that there was no harm in giving him a peek at her lingerie. She unbuttoned her dress and placed it over a chair. She quickly reached for the new dress. Trevor stopped her in her tracks.

"Wait!"

Cheryl looked over at his grinning face. He leered at her while he spoke.

"Wait a second. I want to have a good look."

Cheryl was annoyed, but she allowed him to ogle her for a moment. His eyes undressed her right down to her faux vagina and fake boobs. She was embarrassed by the obvious look. She really despised guys like Trevor but she was pretty much at his mercy. Finally, he gave a motion with his hand for her to continue.

Her initial look at the dress had fooled her. The traditional Aterberry maid uniform was conservative double-breasted attire that buttoned up in front. This uniform zipped up in back and was considerably shorter than the standard outfit. It was also form fitting at the bustline. It was embroidered, with *Housekeeping Cheryl* prominently stitched in bright white. Cheryl struggled with the zipper, giving Trevor a good look at her legs while she wriggled into it. Trevor smiled his approval. Cheryl looked into the mirror and immediately objected.

"I can't wear this, The Aterberry has very modest standards."

Trevor shook his head.

"I already cleared it with Hilda. She told me that you've been too much trouble for her already. She said that you could clean naked for all she cared. Would you rather? I have to say that I would enjoy that too."

Cheryl couldn't believe that she had to wear the new outfit. It was so short that she would have to be mindful of what she was wearing all of the time. Otherwise she would be putting on a suggestive show all day long while she cleaned.

Trevor continued.

"I've ordered several for you so that you have a fresh uniform every day. Now then, show me your appreciation for my gift."

He motioned her over to him by pointing down between his legs. There was no mistaking that movement. Cheryl was totally humiliated. She had given him an eyeful while she changed uniforms. Now, she not only had to go down on him in her skimpy uniform, she had to take his pants down for him in order to do it!

She knelt down in front of him and complied. When she took his cock into her mouth she reminded herself that this time she should check her lipstick before she left his room.

Chapter 43. Home

When Cheryl got home, Robin took a long look at her new uniform.

"I see the Aterberry has changed since I left. I think that I like the new look on you. It brings out your legs and your boobs. How does it feel to be objectified like that?"

Cheryl rolled her eyes.

The new uniform was the start of a whole new relationship with Robin. Cheryl appeared even more feminine than before. In her cute little dress she seemed dainty, not at all like the person she really was underneath all of the feminine trappings. Now Robin viewed Cheryl as not just a maid, but rather, a *lady's* maid. If you have a maid willing to provide intimate services, why not take advantage of that?

It began with little things. Cheryl was required to set out Robin's clothes for her in the morning. Cheryl poured Robin's bath and then toweled her off afterwards. Cheryl even used the blow dryer on Robin's hair for her before brushing her hair for her. Robin took pleasure in the personal attention. She felt like a princess. After all, most women never get to experience the feeling of having a personal maid dote on their every whim.

Giving credence to her lady's maid role, Robin bought little white gloves for her to wear whenever she helped her dress. Robin explained that the gloves were typical attire for maids whenever they engaged in such personal duties.

Back seamed stockings followed. Robin insisted that a fine

maid should wear them. Finally, Robin replaced Cheryl's mob cap with a lace headpiece.

Cheryl had no problem obliging Robin. She relished any excuse to be close to the woman who she adored. The changes simply made her feel more feminine.

Little by little Cheryl became less about providing Robin with oral servitude and more and more about providing traditional maid services. From the moment she came home from work right up until Robin dismissed her for the evening, Cheryl began to fill the role of female maid servant.

For Cheryl it meant cooking, cleaning, and laundry duty. For Robin, it meant an evening of relaxation after a day at work.

They settled into their new roles the way married couples come to settle into theirs. Only their relationship was anything but typical. Now their relationship was completely nonsexual.

Things may never have changed for them, if not for Braxton Brittingham.

Chapter 44. Jackpot

As it turned out, Robin was very successful at her Information Technology internship. She was offered a full-time position, and she quickly accepted it. That was when the owner of the company, Braxton Brittingham, began to notice her.

It began the day when Robin was late for work. She was hurrying to get to her desk when she went around a corner and ran straight into Braxton. Their eyes met and Robin let out a feminine squeal. It was then that Braxton became suspicious. He began to think that the young male intern wasn't what he appeared to be.

From that point on he watched Robin closely. It didn't take long for him to figure out the ruse. Soft silky skin, fine hair, innocent eyes and a feminine walk were all giveaways to the true nature of the intern. He simply deduced the truth. Robin was a girl masquerading as a male in order to work in his company!

He was amused by the charade. If she wanted to work at his company so bad, she could have come in as a girl. He hired girls too! In fact he *mostly* hired girls. So he became interested in why she had disguised herself. He wondered, what was her motivation?

The more he gazed at her the easier it was to see thru her disguise. He could see that she was a beautiful woman hiding behind male clothing. Not only that, but she was witty, intelligent, and interesting to be around. He took to stopping by her desk, then to making sure there was a reason to call her into his office.

It all came to a head the evening that they both worked late. Not together on the same project, just circumstances that caused them to be together in the building long after everyone else had left.

He noticed her working alone at her desk. He invited her for a cup of coffee. He gazed into her eyes.

"You're really a very pretty woman."

Robin was flattered. She blushed. Without thinking, she replied.

"Why thank you…"

Then she realized what she had done. She put her hand over her mouth. Her face blushed pink. He laughed at her embarrassment. He was so casual about his discovery.

"Why the subterfuge Miss Robin?"

She explained that men had taken advantage of her and she would not ever let it happen again.

It was easy for Robin to fall for Braxton. He was everything that Cheryl was not. Even though his slight appearance was similar to Cheryl's, he had other attributes. He seemed romantic to her and intelligent. Obviously he was financially independent. Most importantly, he was understanding and sensitive. What a package he was!

So Robin shared her secret. He noticed her ring. She explained everything about Cheryl. Including that Cheryl was a sissy girl who wore a faux vagina. They hadn't even really consummated their marriage, at least not in the usual way. Robin said that while Cheryl was a good friend, she was not really her type. Cheryl was actually just her maid.

Braxton laughed at the image of the sissy maid in her full uniform fawning over Robin. They laughed together.

Chapter 45. Braxton

It wasn't long before Robin began regularly staying late at work. The more time she spent with Braxton, the closer they became. Having coffee together after hours turned into a daily ritual. Braxton would gaze into Robin's eyes. Her eyes would widen and dance with excitement.

Things changed dramatically when Robin started coming to work dressed more like a woman. First she wore a sheer white nylon blouse over tight black slacks. The outfit gave a hint of the beautiful woman that had been hidden underneath. Then, a few days later, she began wearing alluring dresses. When Braxton saw her in a short, form fitting dress, he knew that he had to get much closer to Robin. She confirmed his desire was well placed by openly flirting with him.

Robin added new sensual clothing to her wardrobe. She took Cheryl with her when she shopped for her new clothes. Cheryl carried Robin's purchases while she continued to shop. Now Robin wore makeup to work and she had her maid apply it for her in the morning. She grew her hair out again and Cheryl fixed it for her every day. There was no question about it, the former male intern was really a beautiful woman.

Braxton liked what he saw. His attractive intern was blooming right in front of his eyes. The more feminine Robin became, the more he desired her. Fate intervened on their relationship and things changed between them for good.

They were working late at night when a storm moved in. With a loud clap of thunder, the power went out in the area. The two of them sat in the dark until Braxton took a small candle out of his desk and lit it up.

Robin and Braxton sat together near the flickering glow of the candle. They talked in whispers about how much they enjoyed the experience of seeing each other in a different light. Finally, Braxton couldn't control his desires any longer. He leaned over to Robin and his mouth found hers in a hungry, passionate kiss.

Robin had no desire to push him away. Instead she returned his kiss with an ardent fervor that left them both breathless. He gripped her in his arms in an embrace that left them both longing for so much more.

His hands found their way under her skirt. He may not have stopped there, but just when she began to moan with desire, there was a flash of lightning and a loud rumble of thunder.

Then the lights came back on.

They both laughed at the timing.

Chapter 46. Dinner and Dessert

The next day, Braxton and Robin went to dinner together. Only they went out for far more than just a meal. In this case dessert was included. They went over to the nearest hotel — The Aterberry — and reserved a room. Then they ordered room service.

Robin was scarcely naïve. She knew that *she* was on the menu. Robin was expecting a long make-out session. Braxton had other more intimate ideas. He could hardly wait to dive into dessert. After dinner, they sat on the bed and they began to kiss.

Robin allowed him to probe her mouth with deep kisses. His hands even found their way underneath her skirt for just a few moments before she pushed him away.

"I'm a married woman Mr. Brittingham!"

He let out a laugh like only a rogue intent on much more could give.

"Mrs. Dearing, certainly you aren't referring to your fake wife are you? Really? You would rebuff me because of your sissy maid? A live-in maid is hardly much of an excuse. Just what did you think was going to happen here tonight?"

Robin flushed with exasperation. A girl should at least be courted properly before she jumped into bed with the first scoundrel who tickled her fancy.

"I expected to share dinner with a gentleman. Then I expected you to take me home. Perhaps if you acted appropriately then there would be a promise of better things to come!"

She lifted her hand to strike his face. He saw it coming, took her hand, and gracefully kissed it. Robin smiled.

"That's much better."

She gave him a soft kiss on his lips.

"I can tell that there is a gentleman hidden somewhere beneath that naughty exterior. Perhaps we can indulge ourselves in dessert another time."

"I look forward to it."

"As do I Mr. Brittingham."

"In that case, my lady, your chariot awaits."

Chapter 47. Apartment Complex

Robin invited Braxton into her apartment for a moment before they said goodnight. Cheryl was back in her bedroom so she didn't hear them when they came in. When Braxton saw the conditions that Robin was living in, he was appalled.

"Robin, how can you live like this?"

"What's wrong with my apartment?"

"It's so…small."

Robin smiled.

"I like to think that it's cozy."

Braxton shook his head.

"I'll not have it. You will move in with me tomorrow."

Robin smiled.

"You sure don't waste any time Mr. Brittingham."

"When I see a damsel in distress, there is no time to waste!"

They both laughed. Robin continued.

"But what of my maid? I can't very well leave Cheryl behind."

He grinned.

"No matter. Bring her along. I have plenty of room and need of another live-in maid. I will employ her at my home. You can both move in."

Robin thought for only a moment. Free lodging, free food, *and* maid service. Plus a rich, dashing gentleman panting for her attributes. Everything a girl could possibly want!

"Why Mr. Brittingham, I don't believe that your intentions are noble."

He feigned hurt feelings.

"I can promise you my lady, they are most assuredly noble. I don't just invite any girl into my home to live with me and my Mother. I can assure you that you will be treated like a fair lady."

"You live with your *Mother*?"

"Yes, I do. But I have to warn you. Mom is a bit… eccentric. But my home is quite large. You won't even know that she is there. I often forget myself."

Again they both laughed. Robin smiled. How much trouble could she possibly get into with his Mother in the house?

"In that case, you have a deal!"

"I'll send movers over in the morning. Have your maid tend to them while you're at work. Afterwards I'll see you home myself. I'm sure that you'll be pleased."

Robin nodded.

"I dare say."

After a passionate goodnight kiss, Braxton was on his way.

Chapter 48. Moving Day

Cheryl was surprised to hear that they were moving out of their apartment. But she had to agree that the opportunity for free food and lodging was far too good to pass up. She would be able to quit her job at The Aterberry and then work full time for Braxton Brittingham at Brittingham House. It was a good opportunity that would get her out of hotel maid employment for good.

Robin gave her simple instructions. Stay with the movers and then go with them to the new place. She would join her after work at Brittingham House. For Cheryl, the excitement built while she waited for the movers. Then her heart fell when she saw them come in the front door.

It was Barry and Greg — the same two guys who had previously stolen from her in her apartment. Barry immediately took notice of the maid uniform that Cheryl was wearing. He glanced over at Greg.

"I see that the pretty girl has a new career. She sure looks as tempting as ever. Hey darlin, do you have any more money?"

He gave an arrogant laugh. The kind of laugh that a villain can make when he knows that he has the upper hand. He knew that a lowly maid couldn't do much to object to anything he might do. Cheryl swallowed hard. She managed to shake her head no. Barry walked right up to her.

"Perhaps this time we should just steal a kiss."

Before Cheryl could react he put his arms around her and pressed his mouth to hers. His tongue forced her lips open before freely probing her at will. One hand found its way down to Cheryl's bottom. Barry pinched her, which caused her to open her mouth wider for her kiss. Greg intruded on the interlude by patting Cheryl on top of her head from behind her.

"Don't worry sweetie pie, we're just supposed to box everything up and deliver it to Mr. Braxton's home. If you ask nicely we won't even wrap you up again."

He laughed at his own joke before continuing.

"We've been well paid, so we won't be taking a thing."

Barry ended his lewd kiss. Cheryl was flushed a deep red. That was so humiliating! Yet what could she possibly say?

The guys brought boxes in and began to pack while Cheryl timidly watched. They continued to leer hungrily at Cheryl while they worked.

Chapter 49. Magic Kingdom

The movers had loaded up the last box. Barry was already sitting in the driver's seat. Greg gave Cheryl a hungry look.

"Missy, do you need a ride?"

Of course she did. She had no other way of getting to Brittingham House where they were taking all of their stuff. She didn't even know where it was.

"Yes please."

Greg smiled. For him it was that much more time to ogle the charming maid.

"All aboard for the Magic Kingdom!"

Cheryl tried to climb into the cab without showing too much leg. Greg was right behind her, no doubt gazing up her dress.

He sat next to her, and he put his hand on her knee. There was no avoiding a certain amount of contact because the front seat of the truck wasn't really built for three. Cheryl squirmed, but she let him rest his hand there. The truck pulled away from the apartment. Then Cheryl tried to ignore him by changing the subject.

"Why did you call Brittingham House the Magic Kingdom?"

Barry took the lead on that question.

"Everybody calls it that. We've moved things in there before. Moved a few things out too."

He chuckled at his joke. Owners can't keep an eye on everything in a place that big!

"The place is massive. It looks like a castle with a gated entrance and a long circular drive to the front portico. It has eight guest rooms, plus two huge suites for Braxton Brittingham and his Mother plus a few suites to spare. There are separate quarters for the servants. It has so many bathrooms I couldn't count them all the last time we were in there.

There's a library, a sitting room, and a game room. Even a pool and tennis courts out back.

I have no idea how many servants live there. I've seen many different maids working there at one time or another. All pretty young girls, just like you. One thing is for sure. I know that Braxton Brittingham enjoys his women and he lives like a King.

The only comparison is that Brittingham House is just like Disneyland. So that's why it's called the Magic Kingdom."

While Barry was talking Greg's hand had worked its way up Cheryl's thigh. She took his hand and removed it before he could feel her up. Barry continued on.

"The gossip is that he has a new girlfriend. I haven't seen her myself but I hear that she is quite a looker. He has had plenty, that's for sure. Money does have its pleasures."

The truck pulled up to the gated entrance. Barry pushed a button on the intercom.

"Movers with a delivery."

A pleasant feminine voice replied.

"Come in. Just follow the drive to the servant's entrance at the back of the house."

With that, the gates slowly swung open. Cheryl couldn't believe where she was going. It was all like a dream.

Chapter 50. Rude Welcome

Cheryl went thru the big doors and stood in the back foyer where she was greeted by a young maid. Outside, the movers were beginning to unload the truck. They were putting all of the boxes on the driveway just behind the moving van before moving them into the house. The maid spoke.

"Stand at attention. Wait for Florence. She's the housekeeping supervisor."

Just then an older woman came down the hallway and walked into the foyer. She came right up to Cheryl and stood in front of her. She looked her up and down with a disapproving eye.

Cheryl thought it best to introduce herself.

"Hi, I'm…"

The woman slapped her face with her right hand. Cheryl's face burned, but she dared not touch her cheek.

"Shut up hussy. If I want you to speak, I'll tell you to speak. Clearly you're the new maid, though you hardly appear it. You look more like a French whore. Who dressed you for work, a cheap pimp? I imagine that you must have previously worked at a bordello. No matter. My son likes to gaze up the dress of the staff, so a tart like you will fit right in."

The woman took her glasses off to get a closer look at Cheryl's *Slave* necklace. She touched it with her fingers while she continued.

"If nothing else, at least you know your place."

She stepped back. Then she noticed Cheryl's ankle bracelet.

"*Slut*? I suppose so. Most girls wouldn't brag about that. I can see that you're proud of yourself, dizzy little tart that you are. Get something straight. If you're here to gold dig, you can forget about it right now. If you turn up pregnant, or if I so much as see you with my son, I'll turn you out into the cold. Do you understand me?"

Cheryl quickly nodded her head.

"Yes."

The woman cringed.

"Such an ill-mannered bitch! You will always address me with *My Lady* and you will curtsy for me when you do so. Need I say more, *stupid* girl?"

"No My Lady."

Cheryl quickly curtsied, just like she had been ordered to do. The woman almost smiled, though she clearly was not the smiling type. Instead, her lips slightly curled up, but then she caught herself.

"Wait here for Florence. She's my House Manager. She'll set you straight. With any luck, I won't have need to teach you ever again."

With that, in somewhat of a huff, the woman turned and walked away.

Chapter 51. Introductions

Cheryl turned to the other maid. She quietly whispered.

"I'm Cheryl. Who was that grouchy woman?"

The maid looked around to make sure that nobody was watching or listening before she spoke.

"I'm Bess. That was Lady Mildred. She's Master Braxton's Mother. Be *very* careful around her. You don't want to end up like the last maid."

Now Cheryl was curious.

"What happened to the last maid?"

"Her name was Tillie. Lady Mildred found her in bed with Master Braxton. He always likes to sample the charms of all of the maids, but Lady Mildred had no clue about it before that. Anyway, she took her by the hand and put her out."

Cheryl smiled.

"That doesn't sound so bad."

"Tillie was naked at the time."

Cheryl cringed.

"Oh dear. What happened after that?"

"I have no idea. I can only imagine. We never heard from her again."

Cheryl wanted to know more.

"You said that Master Braxton samples the charms of all of the maids. Forgive me for asking. Did he, um, sample you?"

"Every night for months. He has quite the appetite for women. Maids in particular. He stopped bedding me when he met a new girlfriend. Her name is Miss Robin. She's been here quite often. A real bitch if you ask me. She looks like a gold-digger. Anyway, after that he lost interest in me. Don't worry, he'll get around to you soon enough. He always does."

Cheryl couldn't believe what she was hearing. Robin was always so nice. Maybe Bess was mistaken. Cheryl let it go and moved on.

"They don't seem to treat you right. Why do you put up with it?"

Bess turned and took a long look at Cheryl.

"Surely you know. I'm sexually submissive, just like you. I'm turned on by the treatment. Mistress Florence looks for that in all of the hires."

Cheryl looked confused. The maid had just met her and she was acting like she knew her. She couldn't help but question the maid's assessment.

"Sexually submissive? I'm not like that. What are you talking about?"

Bess smiled.

"Oh, you don't know much about yourself, do you? I can tell just by looking at you that you'll fit right in. I'll bet you're already excited at the possibilities."

Cheryl realized that Bess was right. Her heart was pounding with anticipation. Plus she had precum seeping into her panties.

Just then the movers came in the doorway with the first group of boxes. Another woman walked up from inside the home at precisely the same moment. She was a tall, imposing, statuesque woman with stiletto heels that enhanced her stature. She looked down on Cheryl from her superior height. She was dressed impeccably in a white satin ruffled blouse with a black leather skirt. The woman spoke in an authoritative tone befitting her attire.

"Bess, show the movers where everything goes. I'll take it from here."

Bess went down the hallway and then up a staircase with the movers trailing close behind. Cheryl overheard Barry make a crude comment regarding Bess's ass. The woman motioned to Cheryl.

"Follow me girl."

Chapter 52. Mistress Florence

They stepped into a small office that was just off the foyer. The woman sat down confidently behind her desk. Since there were no chairs, Cheryl stood in front of her with her hands folded.

"Welcome to Brittingham House. I'm Florence, the House Manager. You will always address me respectfully as Mistress. Do you understand me girl?"

"Yes Mistress."

"I expect a curtsy with that."

Cheryl meekly curtsied. She began to realize that a curtsy was standard fare for Brittingham House.

"Very good. I'll let that go this time. You should know that I run a strict household for Lady Mildred and for Master Braxton. Disrespect, sloppy work, or poor appearance are not tolerated. You are not to speak unless spoken to. You must show deference to your betters at all times. Stand straight, head up, eyes down."

Cheryl complied.

"Very good"

Mistress Florence pointed to a large wooden paddle that was hanging on the wall.

"If I am not satisfied with your performance, you will be punished. I will warn you just once. Punishments are applied with your dress up and your panties down in front of other staff members. You should know that I was a collegiate racquetball champion, so I know how to handle a paddle like a pro. You'll find the experience to be shameful and extremely uncomfortable for days thereafter. I'm sure of that.

Beware. I know you better than you know yourself. Once you've had a taste of the paddle you will find it to be quite addictive. Too many missteps and you'll be yearning for it.

Do I make myself clear?"

"Yes Mistress."

Cheryl wasn't sure if she should, but even though it seemed odd, she curtsied again. She didn't want to be told twice about proper etiquette. Mistress Florence easily commanded that sort of respect so it seemed natural. Mistress continued without a thought about the gesture.

"Very well. I'll speak no more of it. Let's get you started with your duties.

First thing in the morning you will come to my chambers and assist me. I'm up at 6:00 A.M. so you'll need to rise much sooner and get into uniform.

Master Braxton has insisted that you be assigned to Lady Mildred as her personal maid. You will tend to all of her needs."

Cheryl interrupted.

"But I'm Miss Robin's personal…"

Mistress Florence cut her off.

"Impertinent hussy! Haven't you heard a word I've said? Did I ask for your opinion? You haven't even left my office and you've already earned your first punishment! If I want you to serve Lady Mildred, then you will happily serve Lady Mildred with a smile on your face. No questions are to be asked. Immediately after dinner I'll assemble the staff in the basement so that you may learn your first lesson. Do you understand me girl?"

"Yes Mistress."

Cheryl remembered to curtsy again. Mistress Florence smiled at the submissive gesture. There was no doubt about it. The new girl would be easy to dominate. She liked the submissive ones. They made things so much easier for her.

"Very well then. I'm not accustomed to such insolence from the maid staff. Pay attention. I'll continue. Chef Lolita prepares all meals. You will assist Maid Bess in providing breakfast service. After that you will tend to your cleaning duties. Most importantly, linens in all bedrooms are changed daily and every bathroom is made fresh and clean every day. All of the maids are under my charge, but maid Bess will be your immediate supervisor and she will fill you in with further details."

Mistress Florence noticed maid Bess returning with the movers just outside her office.

"Here she is now. You're dismissed. Off with you."

Cheryl almost turned to leave before she caught herself. She gave a little curtsy.

"Thank you Mistress."

Then she went out into the foyer with maid Bess. Florence smiled at the new maid when she walked away. She liked the look of that uniform the new maid wore. Very sexy. Braxton would be suitably tempted.

Chapter 53. Duties

Maid Bess gave Cheryl a long look.

"You look disappointed. Was Mistress in a bad mood today?"

"I'm not sure. But I've been tending to Robin…"

She caught herself before continuing.

"…I mean, I've been serving *Miss* Robin. I had thought that would continue. I've been assigned to Lady Mildred instead."

Bess gave a giggle.

"Good luck with that. I'm glad to be rid of her. She's difficult, to say the least. Not to mention all of those old-fashioned undergarments she wears. She struggles to get in and out of her foundation garments. Don't worry, you'll get used to assisting her."

Cheryl wasn't so sure about that. She had only briefly seen the woman but she had noticed that she was dressed impeccably. Her hair, makeup, and attire were perfect. She realized that the woman most likely hadn't done that on her own. Bess had been responsible for her flawless presentation. Now it would be Cheryl's responsibility.

Bess led Cheryl upstairs at the back of the mansion where the servant's stayed. She took her into a tiny room just big enough for a bed, an armoire, and a dressing table.

"This is your room Cheryl. The bathroom is down the hall. You need to be up early at 6:00 A.M. to tend to Mistress

Florence. Lady Mildred rises at 7:00 A.M. on the dot. Chef Lolita prepares breakfast. We serve at 8:00 A.M. sharp in the dining room. Then we get to our daily duties.

I've been struggling on my own so you'll be a big help. We strip all of the beds every morning, including in the guest rooms, even if they haven't been used. Lady Mildred wants them fresh and ready for company at all times. We'll do that together.

Then you can do the laundry while I dust and vacuum. After the laundry, you can clean the bathrooms while I tend to various other chores. We both serve lunch and dinner together, also in the dining room.

At the end of the day, you assist Lady Mildred as needed. Afterwards you assist Mistress Florence as needed.

Got it?"

Chapter 54. Pecking Order

That first day Cheryl was also introduced to Chef Lolita. Once she saw the elaborate kitchen, Cheryl was glad that she didn't have any cooking duties. She really didn't have very much skill in that area. All she was expected to do was serve meals with Bess and then clear dishes afterwards. Then she was to clean up in the kitchen so that things were ready there for the next meal. That was fine with her.

Chef Lolita was hardly interested in the maids. She gave a wave of her hand to acknowledge their presence before continuing on with her meal preparations.

After they left the kitchen, Bess whispered to Cheryl.

"Rumor has it that Lolita was once seeing Master Braxton. When Mistress Florence came to work here she was reduced to being a chef in the household. At least that was what I heard. I doubt that it is true, but you never know for sure."

Cheryl could picture it. Chef Lolita was a beautiful woman who seemed more suitable to being a fashion model than to be preparing meals at Brittingham House. She wondered how such a beautiful woman found herself working in a kitchen.

It was hardly any of her concern. Bess said that Lolita generally kept to herself. She prepared dishes and then set them out for the maids to serve. If the maids didn't move fast enough, Lolita would scold them for their incompetence. Serving cold food made the chef look bad.

So after meeting Lolita, the pecking order at the Brittingham House was clearly defined in Cheryl's mind. It appeared to her that Lady Mildred was at the top, with Master Braxton and Miss Robin close beneath her. Mistress Florence was in charge of the chef and the maids. Chef Lolita was in charge of the kitchen and she had the maids at her disposal. Bess and Cheryl were at the very bottom of the pecking order along with a few other staff members. Cheryl wasn't terribly surprised. She knew from working at *The Aterberry* that maids were always at the bottom of whatever social ladder might exist at the moment. Hilda had treated her like a slave there so she didn't expect any better than that here. After all, she was just a newly hired junior maid.

Cheryl thought that it must be the uniform. Mistress Florence wore fine clothes, while Lolita had a fancy chef outfit. But Cheryl's attire was just that of a common maid, though admittedly, she wore a uniform with a higher hemline.

The short dress only served to make her appear younger. She knew that would only embolden people to treat her with less respect. The only thing lower than a maid in the household, is a young maid in the household.

Chapter 55. Submission

Initially Cheryl had been excited about serving dinner at Brittingham House. She hadn't seen Robin since she had arrived so it was a chance to be with her again. Things didn't exactly go the way she had hoped.

While Cheryl and Bess served like common maid servants, Robin openly flirted with Master Braxton while an indifferent Lady Mildred observed. In fact, throughout the entire meal, Robin never once even acknowledged the maid. Clearly things had changed between them.

Cheryl could hardly believe it. There she was, within feet of Robin, serving her dinner, and Robin didn't even make eye contact. It was like Cheryl was completely invisible. While it was very unsettling for Cheryl, there was something else that was equally odd.

She also had a strange sense of arousal all evening that was confirmed when she realized that she had dripped precum into her panties. There was something about being treated like a lowly domestic servant that Cheryl found to be intensely erotic. She was so turned on by it all! She hadn't felt that way since the summers that she had spent doing housekeeping chores for her Mother and sister.

She decided that she had to ask Bess what she thought about her strange response to servitude. Once dinner was over the maids were free to talk. While they cleaned up in the kitchen, she told Bess the effect servitude had on her. Bess nodded in understanding.

"Welcome to the club. I told you, submissive personalities are turned on by that sort of treatment. The longer you stay here, the more hooked to the sensation you'll become. Trust me on that."

Cheryl seemed to grasp what Bess was saying.

"What if I want to leave? Can I go?"

"That's the thing Cheryl honey. Mistress Florence won't let you go even if you want to go. She has ways of keeping you here and she can be quite sadistic. Trust me, you really need to stay on her good side or you will regret it later. One maid spent a whole week tied up in the basement being whipped with her riding crop. You don't want that to happen to you. It's miles to the nearest town so you can't walk out of here. Besides, you don't *really* want to go do you? Once you feel the lure of submission it's very hard to say no."

Cheryl could feel the precum dripping in her panties again.

"Florence doesn't look that scary to me."

"She should. She is very pretty but she is also a very dominant woman. I find that I'm completely unable to resist her. What she says, goes."

Bess wanted to tell her everything about Florence, but instead she kept to herself.

Chapter 56. After Dinner

Robin had gone to her bedroom while Cheryl was still finishing up in the kitchen. Braxton sat at the table with his Mother.

"Well Braxton, you finally found yourself a real girl. I was starting to wonder about you. Robin would seem to be quite suitable. Have you put cock to cunt yet?"

"Mother! You do so have a crude way of putting things!"

"Well, I'm not getting any younger. I want grandchildren. She looks to me like she has good child-bearing thighs. You do realize that she wants you, don't you?"

"In due time. Her resistance is fading, I can tell."

"Oh? She's proving hard to get? I'm sure that you'll be in her panties in no time. Nothing wrong with that girl that a good fucking couldn't cure."

"Mother!"

"I'm just saying."

Lady Mildred changed the subject.

"That maid of hers sure seems to enjoy her work. Tell me that you don't have designs on her too. It wouldn't be the first time a horny guy fell for a maid. A sweet thing in a short dress can turn the head of any guy. No doubt you'll soon want to put cock to her too."

"She's not my type."

"Since when? She wouldn't be your first pretty little diversion and I'm sure she won't be your last. You can hardly keep your dick in your pants these days."

"Mom, maid Tillie wasn't what you thought she was. We were dating. I was just getting to know her...more intimately. You just caught us at an inopportune moment."

"Just like all the rest?"

Mildred laughed at the memory of all the girls that Braxton had brought home. He wasn't fooling her at all.

"Perhaps you might act like a gentleman this time. That would be quite a change for you."

Braxton smiled. His Mother had no idea what was going on in her home right under her nose.

He planned on keeping it that way.

Chapter 57. Exposed

Florence was looking forward to teaching the new girl a lesson that she would never forget. The first lesson was always the most important. It would set the tone for future discipline sessions. If the maid accepted the first reprimand, then future punishments would be easy to apply.

Once Bess and Cheryl finished in the kitchen, Florence assembled Lolita, Bess, and Cheryl downstairs in the basement. It was a dingy, dimly lit space, that had overtones of a medieval dungeon.

Florence knew that the first spanking was a test for all of the new maids. Tillie had yearned for the paddle because she was submissive too. Tillie had remained even after her first punishment session. Other maids left the following morning. With their bottoms still stinging, they were far too humiliated to stay. Sexual submission is not for everyone.

Bess stood at attention. She was thinking about her first spanking. That was when she discovered how submissive she was. Mistress Florence had been magical with her paddle. She had brought Bess to the brink of orgasm twice before she finally allowed Bess to climax with a final swift swat on her bare bottom. The feeling was sexually thrilling, shamefully embarrassing, totally addictive, and sheer delight. Her body tingled just thinking about it.

Bess glanced at Cheryl. She knew that she was submissive. She could tell. She still wondered what her reaction to the paddle would be. Would she orgasm quickly, or would it take time? Would Mistress Florence toy with her or tan her bottom a deep red? The speculation was deliciously tantalizing. Bess found her own excitement had raised her own heartbeat. She wanted to touch herself in her special place, but she knew better than to do that in front of Mistress Florence. The Mistress had forbidden self-gratification.

Cheryl stood at attention in front of Florence. Cheryl realized that she had messed up earlier in the day. She didn't really think that the Mistress was going to follow thru on her threat to spank her. But the Mistress had the paddle that Cheryl had seen in her office in her hand at the ready.

"Ladies, as you know we don't put up with any nonsense here at Brittingham House. The impertinence of our new maid must be dealt with. We can't have her forming bad habits. Bess, silence her."

Maid Bess knew the drill. She already had a penis gag in her hand. She walked up to Cheryl while Florence taunted the maid.

"Open wide girl. This is your chance to practice sucking cock."

Lolita grinned. She always liked seeing a new maid get her comeuppance. It was always a real treat to witness a new maid being put in her place. The slut would never be the same once Mistress Florence had her way with her. A red bottom always had a way of putting a girl in her place. Served her right.

Cheryl immediately obeyed. She wanted to laugh. After servicing Mr. Tolworth, a penis gag would be no trouble at all. Bess fastened it in place before Florence continued.

"Now girl, lower your panties for your spanking."

Cheryl hesitated for a moment. She had thought that Mistress Florence was joking when she said she would be paddled on her bare bottom. But it was true! She knew that even in the low light of the basement that Mistress Florence would be able to get a good look at her. She would be able to see that she was wearing a fake vagina under her panties.

Florence was annoyed by her delay.

"You were to get ten of my best. But now you've dawdled. I think that twenty would be more appropriate."

Cheryl quickly reached under her dress and lowered her panties before her Mistress decided to add any more.

"Lift your dress girl. With both hands."

This time the sissy immediately complied. Florence went moved closer to her, paddle in hand. Suddenly she stopped.

"My, my, my. What have we *here*?"

Florence gave a little tug at the top of the fake vagina. She instantly knew exactly what it was.

"Ladies, somebody has been dishonest with us. I think we have a *sissy* girl here. Sissy girl, take the rest of it down too."

Cheryl knew that she had no choice. She struggled a bit with the tight silicon garment but in the end it was down at her ankles just like her panties. Her tiny sissy clit was finally free. It immediately sprung to life, pointing straight up in all of its gorged excitement.

Bess opened her mouth in complete amazement. Lolita and Florence both giggled at the obscene reaction of the little penis. A grinning Florence continued, this time with a derisive tone.

"No wonder our maid pretends to be a girl. With that little thing no one could possibly tell the difference. Look ladies, she is excited about the prospect of being spanked. What a sissy! We'll be able to have loads of fun with this one."

Florence touched the paddle to the tip of the erect penis. She gave it a playful nudge that caused it to twitch with excitement. Florence laughed at the lewd spectacle.

"Now I understand why you wear that ankle bracelet. What a slut!"

All of the ladies laughed. Cheryl turned a deep shade of embarrassed red. She wanted to run away and hide, but where would she go? She knew better than to disobey Mistress Florence. So instead, she stayed at attention, holding her dress up exposing both her bottom and her firm erection.

Mistress Florence noticed that the sissy was beginning to drip precum. She snapped at Bess.

"Girl, I'm sure Master Braxton taught you how to properly suck cock. Take it in, but don't you dare excite the sissy."

Bess knew that disobedience would bring immediate punishment. So she quickly dropped to her knees and took the petite erection into her mouth. It was so diminutive that her lips easily gently caressed the base of the obscene rod. Compared to Master Braxton, this was a very small specimen indeed. She was balls deep and the tip of the penis wasn't even close to her throat. Cheryl moaned with arousal at the warmth of the maid's mouth.

Lolita was totally amused at the scene of Bess kneeling before the sissy maid with the maid's cock deep in her mouth. Florence was just beginning to have her fun. She hadn't played with a sissy girl in quite some time so she was really going to enjoy this. Sissy girls were definitely the easiest to humiliate.

Chapter 58. Punishment

Florence spoke in an authoritative tone so that the sissy would get the message.

"I'm going to apply your twenty now. If you come in Bess's mouth, I'll add twenty more. Do you understand me sissy girl?"

Cheryl couldn't speak with the penis gag in her mouth, so she simply nodded her head. Florence took aim and with a swing of her arm she landed the first strike with everything that she could summon.

Cheryl jumped at the sting of the paddle and pressed her cock further into Bess's mouth in the process. Making intimate contact with Bess like that served to arouse her further. The second blow was just as firm, yielding the same results.

Mistress Florence knew precisely what she was doing. She was having Bess give the sissy a paddle-powered blowjob. If she was lucky, the sissy girl would lose her erection from the pain and then she would only get twenty. If not, then Bess would get a mouthful and Cheryl would get twenty more. It was win-win!

By the tenth stroke Cheryl was in serious pain. Her bottom stung from the paddle. At the same time she was trying to suppress her arousal. She couldn't believe the erotic humiliation that she was feeling. Bess could feel the climax welling up inside the penis that was resting gently between her lips. Bess began to weakly signal no with her head in an attempt to keep Cheryl from sending ejaculate gushing into her open mouth. She had tasted semen before, and it was not a taste that she ever wanted to experience again.

Florence and Lolita both grinned at the helpless scene of total submission that was playing out right in front of them. The sissy girl was willingly accepting her spanking. She was even turned on by it! Bess was about to reluctantly accept a mouthful of semen. Neither one of the two submissive maids had the willpower to put a stop to the embarrassing humiliation that Mistress Florence was gleefully administering.

Mistress Florence paused for a moment. She ran her hand over the maid's red-hot bottom before she taunted the maid.

"Oh, tsk, tsk, tsk! Your ill-disciplined bottom is *so* red! Such a naughty, naughty girl! I doubt that I could possibly make it any redder than that. Whatever should I do with you? Well, I'll just have to give it a try."

She laughed heartily before continuing with the punishment.

Cheryl almost managed to last the twenty swats before she had the orgasm of a lifetime. But it was not to be. The sissy penis remained seductively teased in Bess's mouth. Cheryl tried her best not to become too excited. But it was useless. At seventeen swats, with Bess frantically begging incoherently for the sissy to stop, Cheryl pumped her excitement into her waiting mouth. Florence continued to apply three more stinging swings of the paddle while the sissy continued to thrust forward until she was fully spent.

Bess had no choice. Her mouth filled with warm semen until she was forced to swallow it. Then she sucked on the penis in order to make sure that the spurting fluid went into her mouth — she didn't want any cum to drip on her uniform.

Lolita applauded in appreciation of the bawdy spectacle that Florence had provided for her amusement. Not only had Cheryl been completely humiliated, but Bess had received her just desserts too.

Florence paused for just a moment. After Bess swallowed every last drop of cum the Mistress continued with the remainder of the assigned punishment. Twenty more! Only now the sissy girl was no longer aroused so the pain and the shame that came with it were both intensified.

At least Bess was more comfortable. She still had that awful taste of semen in her mouth, but the cock had shrunk to a little nubbin that she could barely manage to keep her lips on. But she knew better than to let it go, so she sucked on it a bit to keep it in place. She stayed in position while the remainder of the punishment was administered.

When Florence finished with them, she told them both to stay in right where they were. Then she set a timer for thirty minutes. She told them they could move on once it went off. With that, Lolita and Florence left them to contemplate their shame.

Chapter 59. Setting The Tone

The next morning Master Braxton summoned Mistress Florence to his office. Similar to the rest of the mansion, his home office was opulent. Plush carpeting, elaborate bookcase, and built-in bar highlighted his amenities. He sat behind his mahogany desk in a fine leather chair when Mistress Florence entered. Just like her own office, there was no chair for Florence to sit in so she stood in front of him with her hands folded.

"I understand that you have discovered the truth about our new maid."

"Yes I have, Master Braxton. I had no idea that she was a sissy maid."

Braxton gave her a sly smile.

"You may dispense with the formalities Florence. There is nobody close by. You know that's just for appearances. This is personal. In private, I am just Braxton and you are Mistress Florence. Right?"

Florence was flattered. She liked it when Braxton remembered their actual relationship and pointed it out himself. They had worked hard to keep their secret. It had been some time since Braxton had talked in private with such casual conversation outside of his bedroom.

"Of course I knew about the sissy maid. The thing is, I want Miss Robin for my own. You can appreciate that, can't you?"

Of course she could. Florence could hardly forget that she

was once the sole object of Braxton's affection. He had made love to her every night for months. What a lover he was! His libido was insatiable. He was everything a girl could possibly want in a good fucking.

She had cried when he broke up with her for another woman. It was unbelievable. The new girl was a mere maid! Florence had begged Braxton to stay on. He had accommodated her by offering her a job. That's how she became House Manager. It was only then that she discovered her true power. Since then, Braxton had fucked just about every pretty girl he could find. She didn't particularly mind anymore. She actually had the upper hand. She smiled.

"Yes, I can appreciate the situation. I understand fully. What can I do to help?"

"Please do not share any of this conversation with anyone, particularly with Miss Robin. It is of utmost importance that you keep our little talk a secret. Our sissy maid is smitten with my wife-to-be. I'll not have a sissy stand in my way. I can't have another cock, as puny as it may be, anywhere near my love. It will never do."

Florence nodded.

"I can see the problem, though I must say, it *is* a rather small one."

"Be that as it may, I'm sure that you can still see the complication. For whatever reason, Miss Robin does have an affinity for this particular sissy girl, so I can only see one possibility."

Florence was curious. She could think of more ways to deal with this than just one.

"Oh?"

"I'm counting on you Florence. I intend to make a woman of our sissy maid. Then I want you to get rid of her. A lifetime working at The Aterberry ought to do her good. She'll make a fine chamber maid. A few years of making beds and cleaning toilets should soften her libido. They owe me over there. See to it. I don't ever want to see her again. I don't want her fawning over Miss Robin, that's all. I want you to see to it that she'll never be able to have her like I will."

Florence licked her lips. This was becoming far more interesting than she could have ever imagined.

Braxton reached into the top desk drawer and took out a couple of prescription bottles.

"These will get her started. Put them into vitamin containers and give them to the sissy girl. Tell her that she looks tired and that they are vitamins to be taken every day. I've got more on order, they'll come to your attention. I can provide you with refills when needed."

Florence took the pills in her hand.

"There's no label on these. What are they?"

Braxton grinned.

"No matter. If she takes them in a week or so she'll be left with a cock so limp that she'll be unable to perform under any circumstance. It will only be the first step for our sissy girl. Eventually, I'll have you call Doctor Carter and she'll do the rest."

Florence fully understood the implication. She was quite familiar with Doctor Elizabeth Carter. She would have supported Braxton regardless of his intentions, but this was absolutely delicious. Florence smiled.

"The sissy is dressed like a woman. It is only fitting that she become one."

They both laughed.

Braxton handed Florence several legal documents.

"Have her sign these, but don't let her read them. There is an employment contract with Brittingham House on the top and an employment contract with The Aterberry on the bottom. But in between there are agreements to rename her Cheryl Meeks, divorce papers, and consent to gender re-assignment surgery. There are also papers making you her legal guardian with full power of attorney in all matters. If you do that for me I would be *extremely* grateful."

Florence smiled. That was what she wanted to hear.

"Just *how* grateful would you be Braxton?"

She gave him her most sensual look. Before he replied she lifted her dress slightly and smoothed her stocking. Brandon grinned.

"Come to my bedroom tonight after everyone has gone to sleep. You can have whatever you want. I think that I can satisfy *all* of your needs."

She smiled.

"Oh, you most certainly will."

Chapter 60. Florence and Braxton

The mansion was quiet when Florence tip-toed into Braxton's dimly lit bedroom. Everyone had gone to sleep except for Florence and Braxton. He was laying naked on his bed while she was still dressed in her white blouse and her leather skirt. In addition, she was wearing black leather gloves. He couldn't see what she was carrying, but she placed something on the dresser and walked up to the bed.

"You said that I could have *anything*, right?"

"Yes Mistress Florence. Anything that you want."

"Do you mean it? You *know* I play rough."

"Absolutely."

Braxton gave Florence a hungry stare. The kind of stare a child might make when he was too scared to take a piece of candy in front of his Mother. Naughty boys know better.

Florence whispered with a stern authority that only an experienced Dominatrix could possibly have.

"On your knees slave!"

Braxton got out of bed and quickly crawled over to her on his knees. He put his head down at her feet just like she had always instructed him to do before. From there he had a close-up look at her beautiful ankles encased in fine stockings. He always found Florence to be irresistible, and when she spoke with an air of authority he melted in the aura of her feminine power. Florence wasn't just a remarkable House Manager and a great fuck. He had learned the hard way that she was a fine Dominatrix and that she knew precisely how to put a man in his place. His apparent position at the head of the household was actually quite a ruse kept up solely for appearances. In truth Florence was in charge. He didn't dare to disobey her.

"Very good slave. Don't move."

She went to the dresser and picked up the object she had brought in with her. Then she knelt down behind him. Using her gloved hand she pulled his cock and balls back between his legs. Braxton knew what was coming. He begged with a timid voice.

"Please Mistress, not the Humbler."

"Oh yes my slave, that is precisely what you are going to get tonight. I insist. You said anything that I want. I want the Humbler, just for you."

For those unfamiliar with the Humbler, also occasionally called the Hanson Humbler, the device is the ultimate in imposing female superiority. The Humbler forces the male to stay bent over or kneeling by holding his cock and testicles between his legs behind him. They are held in place by the Humbler--two pieces of wood or metal that lock together with a strategically placed hole for the scrotum. The victim has his cock pulled tight between his legs and his balls are then held securely in plain view.

The effect is a stunning display of absolute female domination. Once locked in place, the Humbler has the ability to render a male completely helpless. The male is unable to stand while his most intimate sensitive parts are lewdly displayed, readily accessible for feminine amusement. The tugging on the testicles increases should the male even attempt to try to stand up, effectively keeping him bent over. The victim is in the perfect position to take whatever punishments that a dominant woman might desire to give him.

The victim looks utterly ridiculous being tethered in such a demeaning pose. He is held securely in place that way by his cock and balls. You might say the victim is completely humbled, forced to kneel at the feet of a powerful woman. Thus the device is termed the Humbler.

An entertaining sequence of ball slapping, testicle squeezing, and amusing ball fondling typically follows while the powerless victim pleads helplessly for mercy. Such torture is applied strictly at the whim of the woman in charge. The subject is unable to resist whatever his captive cares to administer.

Florence was quite familiar with the Humbler. It was one of her favorite toys. Naturally she had used it many times before on Braxton. Braxton moaned with arousal while Florence handled his cock and balls, his male arousal keeping him from attempting to evade certain torture. She pulled his cock back between his legs into the perfect position for the Humbler to be applied. Then she secured his balls with the Humbler, locking him into position on his knees. He knew that any attempt to resist by trying to get up would result in a very painful tug on his testicles. He begged for mercy while she laughed at his pitiful attempt to dissuade her.

"Please Mistress, please…"

"You horny toad. What a slut you are. I'll teach you to bring another woman into this household."

With the Humbler in place he was completely at her mercy. She took off one of her gloves and with one swift movement she slapped his balls. He yelped in pain. His erection immediately vanished. She tightened the Humbler a bit to take up the slack.

"Please Mistress, please don't…"

There was another quick smack with her leather glove. Florence taunted him in a mocking girlish tone. She wanted him to feel like it had only taken a girl to completely dominate him and that he was at her feminine mercy.

"Oh dear me. Do Braxie Waxie's tiny little ballsie wallsies hurt?"

She slapped his balls again. This time, he let out a more painful sound. Just then the door to the bedroom opened and Robin came in.

"I thought I heard…"

She stopped and gaped at the scene of the Dominatrix torturing Braxton. Florence grinned at her.

"Certainly you didn't think that *he* was in charge here, did you?"

In the position that he was in, Braxton couldn't see Robin, but he could tell by the sound of her voice that Robin had come into the room. Realizing how it must look to her, and that Robin had no idea what was going on, Braxton tried to talk.

"Robin, I can explain…"

Florence took a dildo gag out of her skirt pocket and stuffed it into his mouth. She fastened it securely behind his head.

"Braxton won't be explaining anything tonight honey. He has his mouth full of cock at the moment. He seems to have lost track of his place in the household. I'm giving him an attitude adjustment tonight. Perhaps you would care to join in and further explain it to him?"

She offered Robin her leather glove. Robin took one look at Braxton's predicament and she immediately got into the spirit of it. She took the glove from Florence and then gave his balls another taste of the leather. He howled in pain beneath his gag.

Both ladies sat on the bed. Then they had Braxton position himself at their feet. He moved very carefully, trying not to give himself any more pain than was absolutely necessary. Finally he kneeled before both of them, with his head down at their feet. Florence removed his gag. Since Robin had already decided to join in, there was no longer a need for it. Florence snapped a command.

"Slave lick my feet."

Braxton immediately complied. Florence was wearing strappy heels so her toes were readily accessible. He lapped away at her toes while the ladies casually talked. Florence began the discussion.

"I told my slave that he was going to need approval from me before he brought another woman into this house. He did not ask permission to bring you in, so I am punishing him tonight.

I realize that you may not fully understand. So let me explain. Braxton is a submissive male. We were intimate lovers until he spurned me for another of his tawdry conquests. She was a slut who has since moved on. Once I discovered his submissive nature and his fetish for female stockings, heels, and a well-turned ankle, well, now he's my sex slave. Now *I* am in charge of Brittingham House.

The truth is that he receives sexual pleasure from giving sexual pleasure to women. He would much rather give you an orgasm than to experience one of his own. All submissive males are like that."

Robin smiled.

"So I see. He is a bit more submissive than I thought that he could possibly be. Is he always like that?"

"Oh, he is very submissive alright. I've trained him well. He'll do just about anything that a woman commands him to do. Isn't that right slave?"

A meek voice responded.

"Yes Mistress."

"Lick Robin's heels."

Robin was surprised that he obediently began to lick her black patent heels. She immediately regretted that she hadn't been wearing her strappy heels. She would have liked to have enjoyed the feel of his tongue on her toes.

"See how obedient he is?"

"I'll say. I would have never thought."

"It has been necessary to conceal his true servile temperament.

He has quite the appetite for women. You might say his appetite is insatiable. Any dominant woman who knows the truth about him can order him to pleasure her and he simply can't resist. He is helpless in the presence of an authoritative woman. Isn't that right slave?"

Again there was a timid reply.

"Yes my Mistress."

Florence turned her attention back to Robin.

"Female sexual power is the most potent force on earth. Once you realize that, there's nothing you can't do with a male. They are helpless before our sensual supremacy. I've found that it really is quite erotic to be in charge. In order for Braxton to successfully run his company I've kept his true nature a secret. He knows the truth. The purpose of the male is to pleasure women, isn't that right slave?"

"Yes my Mistress."

Robin couldn't believe what she was hearing, but she liked the sound of it. A male who agreed that his lot was to pleasure women? How unexpected! How wonderful! Florence continued.

Have you ever had your ass licked?"

Florence sounded so nonchalant about ass licking. Robin was a bit taken aback by such casual manner. Finally Robin shook her head.

"No, I can't say that I have."

"Well, you're in luck tonight!"

"But first, you have to try out his tongue in an even better place. He likes to worship pussy, don't you dear?"

Braxton paused licking Robin's heels just long enough to reply.

"Yes Mistress."

Florence smiled with delight.

"Allow me to demonstrate."

Chapter 61. Oral Servitude

Robin watched in awe while Florence removed Braxton's Humbler. His limp cock had been completely subdued by the device. He stayed obediently in position while Florence fastened his wilted cock into a penis chastity. Precum dripped from Braxton's flaccid penis. Clearly he was still aroused by his treatment, but he was unable to show it with an erection. Apparently the ball slapping had reduced his manhood to a harmless appendage. Florence noticed the look on Robin's face so she explained.

"Did you notice before I put him in chastity that he didn't become erect? A wilted penis in the company of two attractive women is proof positive of his total submission. He is so obedient that he can't even get a stiffy in our presence. That's complete and total surrender to my female authority. You should also know that he is not allowed to ejaculate without my permission. Putting his cock in chastity will enforce my decree."

Once he was fully restrained Florence stood in front of the subdued slave.

"Undress me slave."

Robin had never seen such a display of adoration that followed. Braxton carefully removed Florence's clothing, but not quickly the way most males might tear at a woman's clothing. No, Braxton respectfully removed each garment, then folded it tenderly, before reverently placing it aside.

Robin stared at Florence's nudity while Braxton delicately placed Florence's panties on the dresser. The Mistress was stunningly attractive. She was exquisitely beautiful with curves in all the right places. Robin could only imagine how gorgeous the maid must have been for Braxton to give up such a magnificent woman for her. Florence's pubes were shaved clean. They glistened noticeably from her wetness. Florence observed her interest.

"I shaved them because it intensifies the pleasure. If you haven't tried it, you should. You'll be quite pleased. I know that I am."

She sounded so nonchalant about shaving her pubes, like every woman naturally does it! Robin had never considered such a thing. Florence positioned herself comfortably on the bed. She gave a casual glance at Braxton.

"Slave, pleasure me."

Her devoted servant obediently approached. He was in no rush. His adoration was plainly evident. His tongue started at her neck before systematically moving down and gently finding her nipples.

Robin found herself incredibly aroused from the image. She had never before seen a male reduced to a mere slave used solely to provide a woman pleasure. Such a wonderful delight! When Florence moaned with desire, Robin felt a twinge deep inside that told her that she wanted to be pleasured too.

Soon Braxton's face was buried between Florence's legs. She met his tongue with hips thrust upwards in a hungry attempt to increase her own pleasure. He accommodated her, lapping obediently, yet slowly, in order to maximize her inevitable orgasm.

What followed was heavenly. Florence would scream with pleasure, not once, but twice before she passed out from her orgasmic exertion. Only then did he stop tending to her needs.

Chapter 62. Robin's Turn

With Florence completely satiated, Braxton turned his attention to Robin. She could detect the fragrance of Florence's musk while he methodically undressed her. She was dripping with excitement when she placed herself on the bed, right next to Florence. The house manager was still sound asleep when Braxton began to work his magic on her firm nipples.

Robin had no time for foreplay. She pushed his head down towards her love nest. He resisted. Instead he made little circles around her nipples with his tongue, driving her into a sexual frenzy.

Robin lost all control. For the first time in her life she willingly surrendered her sexuality. She writhed in sensual delirium while he played with her like she was a violin in a symphony. He played her up and down the scales, all leading up to the ultimate climax. She didn't want him to ever stop. She wanted him to take her wherever his tongue was lapping towards without delay.

The time neared for the ultimate crescendo. Not a moment too soon for her yearning body. He gently tended to her dire needs between her legs while she begged him to continue. She breathlessly warned him that she would whip him if he stopped. She lost track of her surroundings. She had no idea where she was. She only knew the euphoria that was radiating from deep inside her that made her body tingle from head to toe. She didn't care if what was happening was right or if it was wrong. She just wanted it to happen.

What a climax it was! When she finally screamed in a fit of orgasmic frenzy, he continued to slowly tongue her until her waves of passion subsided. Then he paused for a moment before starting all over again. Robin had ceded ultimate control to the sex slave who was taking her to heaven. She was more than willing to go.

Florence woke up the second time Robin orgasmed. Robin had no clear recollection of what happened after that. With her passion fully drained, her mind was lost in a cloud of bliss.

Later she vaguely remembered hearing Florence say something and then she recalled the sensation of a tongue lapping away at her bottom. The tongue lingered at her perineum in a delightful helping of sensual dessert. She had never been teased there like that, so it was a whole new idyllic sensation. She found the feeling to be exceptionally pleasing.

After that she fell into a deep sleep. Her last thought was that she hoped nobody would find out in the morning that she had spent the night naked in Braxton's bed. She didn't want anyone to think that she was that kind of girl.

Even if she was.

Chapter 63. A New Light

When Robin finally woke up, the sun was brightly streaming in through the window in Braxton's bedroom. Braxton had already gone off to work. Florence was downstairs tending to her duties.

Robin's entire body was sore from her exertion the night before. Her whole body felt the strain of the thrilling sexual adventure. The pleasure had certainly been worth the discomfort. Even though her slave had licked her sex clean the night before, she made her way to the shower. While the warm water brought her to life, she lathered up her pubes and then shaved herself clean. There was no sense in waiting to find out if Florence was right about a shaved pussy. She wanted to experience even greater euphoria, though she doubted that was possible. Yet she was more than willing to give it try.

Robin saw Braxton in a whole new light while Bess was dressing her. She had no idea that Braxton was so submissively inclined. She had been fooled by his romantic advances and his apparent devotion.

The night before he had given her the very best oral servitude that she had ever experienced. His tongue made Cheryl's feel like that of a little adolescent girl. Clearly he was more experienced in such matters. Robin had been satisfied unlike ever before. Her mind glowed with possibilities.

What was she to do with Braxton Brittingham? Clearly he was head over heels in love with her. She knew that he would fuck her brains out if given half a chance. But then most likely he would discard her like the other women he had bedded.

Before she didn't want to give in to him. Now she realized that perhaps she didn't have to.

The thought of being in charge of Braxton was extremely appealing. It was one thing to dominate Cheryl, but quite another to dominate Braxton. If his performance the night before was any indication, he would make a fine sexual slave.

Cheryl was a different story. Cheryl was a timid sissy girl. She was hardly worth keeping around for anything other than housekeeping duty. But Braxton! He was a real find, with a delightfully eager tongue. He was romantic and sensitive. Yes, he was cocky. She knew he couldn't keep his penis to himself. But he sure had an adorable tongue. With proper supervision he could make a fine conquest.

For the first time in her life she realized that a woman could be dominant in the bedroom. She didn't have to surrender to the cravings of a male. She could be in charge just like she had been the night before. She loved the feeling.

If she married Braxton, she would have him at her disposal, she could retain her virginity, and she could take charge of his fortune. She could keep Florence on to run the household. Florence could help her with things in the bedroom that she didn't know how to do.

She daydreamed about games she could play with her adoring slave. She would have him bring her to a luscious orgasm every night. Maybe even two orgasms! A cock is seldom up for two orgasms, but a tongue! Maybe even three! Why not?

Bess helped her into her panties. The fine nylon felt different directly against her soft, shaved, sensitive skin. Her sex was tenderly caressed in an erotic fabric that gently fondled her.

She had never thought of nylon panties to be a sensual treat. It was a whole new carnal tease that she immediately began to enjoy.

She licked her lips while Bess zipped her into her dress. She wore a tiny little red number today. She wanted to tease Braxton. After all, he must be as horny as hell. Even after her sexual exploits the night before *she* certainly was. So he had to be. Florence never let him orgasm last night. She would tease him today as best as she could.

It would be fun. With his cock secured in its cage, there would be nothing that he could do to satisfy himself. Her new slave would long for her body, but he would be unable to take it. How luscious that would be!

Her thoughts were interrupted by maid Bess.

"Miss Robin, which heels would you care to wear today?"

Robin smiled.

"The strappy red heels, please."

The maid went to the closet to get them. Then she gently placed them on Robin's feet.

Chapter 64. Signing

Florence had told Cheryl to report to her office right after
serving breakfast. Cheryl was already exhausted even though
it was early in the morning. She had been up late cleaning in
the kitchen the night before and she still wasn't accustomed to
getting up early to dress Mistress Florence. Her bottom still
stung from the spanking she had at Florence's hand. She
found the sensation to be exciting in an odd sort of way.

It had been erotic dressing her supervisor. Mistress Florence
wore a frilly, lacy, bra and panty set worthy of a fine woman.
Cheryl felt privileged to be able to tend to her in such an
intimate manner. She tried to maintain a proper attitude
when she clipped Mistress into her bra. It had not been easy
to do. Mistress Florence was a beautiful woman. Her
professional outfit hardly did her figure justice. She had seen
that for herself.

The maid stood at attention in front of Florence's desk. Cheryl
noticed that the paddle that had hung harmlessly on the wall
was now on top of Mistress Florence's desk. Next to the
paddle was a small stack of papers along with a couple of
bottles of pills.

Florence smiled at the maid.

"Lady Mildred told me that you looked tired. We can't have
that now, can we? I've got vitamins for you. Take one of each
of these every day. I also have your employment contract. It's
fairly standard, you may read everything if you want, or you
may just quickly sign these papers and then be off to your
duties. I hardly have time to explain anything to you so be
quick about it."

Florence moved her hand over to the paddle. It was hardly a veiled threat. It didn't take Cheryl long to decide what she wanted to do. Cheryl looked at the paddle and then she looked at the papers. Sign immediately or face the paddle! How much harm could the papers possibly be? She quickly signed each of the pages without giving them even a glance. Florence tried to contain her glee.

"Well done girl. One more thing. Lady Mildred doesn't like her servant wearing a wedding ring. She wants your attention solely on her needs. Please hand it over."

Cheryl thought it to be an odd request, but she turned her ring over to Florence anyway. Florence smiled.

"Very good. I'll keep this for you. No loitering about. Now off to your chores."

"Yes Mistress."

Without even thinking Cheryl curtsied. It was already becoming a habit.

Florence held the ring in her hand for a few moments while Cheryl left the room. She was pleased with her improvisation. She hadn't thought to take the ring until that very moment. The maid was so gullible! The girl had no idea what was to become of her. Perhaps it was better that way.

Florence took a close look at the ring. Just like she had suspected, it was a worthless fake diamond ring.

Cheryl wouldn't be needing the ring anymore. Florence tossed the ring into the garbage can.

Chapter 65. A Week Later

Cheryl realized that Florence had been right. She could still feel the sting of her paddle a full week later. Simply sitting down remained a painful experience and a reminder of the humiliation that she had endured. She also had a craving for the intense orgasm that had come with it. The strange thing was that she couldn't seem to get an erection. It was an odd feeling. She had a passionate desire but she couldn't seem to put it to use. Instead, her faux vagina kept her cock safely secured in a manner that, from outside appearances, gave her a resemblance of a real woman. For some reason that gave her comfort.

She disregarded the peculiar feeling. She reasoned that it was simply because of all of the housework that she was doing that she didn't have enough energy left to even excite herself.

That morning, she got another surprise when Bess came in to help her with their daily ritual of providing fresh bed linens. Bess appeared wearing the same uniform that Cheryl wore, complete with necklace, ankle bracelet, and back-seamed stockings. *Housekeeping Bess* was embroidered in unmistakable lettering on her dress.

"Bess, what are you wearing today?"

"Thanks a lot Cheryl. Florence thought it would be amusing if we both looked the same so she got me the same uniform that you have. How can you possibly wear this every day? I feel like a French whore!"

Cheryl shrugged her shoulders.

"I guess you just get used to it."

"When Master Braxton sees me in this, I'll be in trouble for sure."

Cheryl smiled. She knew exactly what Master Braxton would do.

"In trouble on your backside!"

Both girls laughed before Bess continued.

"He's quite the lover. His cock can touch a girl…"

She blushed before continuing.

"I guess that I shouldn't talk like that. I forgot for a moment that you're not a real maid."

Cheryl disagreed.

"Don't think of me like that. Treat me just like you would any other maid. I promise you that I won't take advantage of you."

Bess rolled her eyes. She didn't really believe the sissy.

"You *are* somewhat of a sissy girl. You'll have to forgive me though, because I've never had another maid cum in my mouth."

Cheryl remembered her spanking and being so excited that she had ejaculated into Bess's mouth.

"I'm so sorry Bess. It wasn't my fault. You saw how it happened."

"I sure did. I had to take that tiny little thing of yours into my mouth and suck on it. It was disgusting!"

"I'm so sorry Bess. How can you ever forgive me?"

Bess looked at Cheryl. The maid seemed *so* sincere. Imagine apologizing for ejaculating into her mouth! She never knew a guy who would do *that*. Bess decided that Cheryl really was a sissy girl. That gave Bess an idea.

"There is something that you can do to make it up to me."

Cheryl brightened up. Bess was becoming her best friend and she would do anything to keep her happy.

"What would you like? Anything you want!"

Bess smiled.

"Well, because of you I have to wear this tawdry outfit. The least that you can do is help me out of it tonight after work."

Cheryl quickly agreed.

Chapter 66. Bess Undressed

Bess had never been tended to by a maid before, let alone a sissy maid. She had always thought that only the lady of the house could be served like that. When Cheryl started to help her undress she felt like a queen.

Cheryl was still becoming accustomed to being in such close proximity to such attractive women. Helping Lady Mildred out of her foundation garments was one thing, but assisting Mistress Florence was quite another. Now she was helping Bess out of her uniform. She hadn't realized it before, but once the maid was out of uniform Cheryl could see that she too was a magnificent vision of womanhood.

For just a moment Cheryl gaped at Bess. Bess was only dressed in her bra, panties, and her back-seamed stockings. She was quite alluring to say the least. Bess caught her gazing at her.

"I thought you said that you wouldn't take advantage of me?"

"I'm so sorry. I couldn't help it. You're so beautiful."

Bess smiled.

"Thank you. I needed that. But tonight you are my lady's maid. You are to treat me like you do Lady Mildred. I expect you to be obedient, respectful, and most grateful to be my servant. Now pour me a bath."

The bathroom was right next to Bess's room. While all of the bedrooms had private baths, including Florence's, the maids shared one bath at the end of the hallway. Since she was senior maid, it was a small perk for Bess to be located so close to it. Cheryl quickly set to pouring a bath for Bess.

Just when the tub was about filled, Bess walked into the bathroom. She was really enjoying her special night. She tried to sound snooty.

"Undress me girl!"

Cheryl carefully helped her out of her stockings. Then she lowered her panties before unclipping her bra.

It took all of the self-control that the sissy could muster not to ogle the nude woman who stood before her. She tried to act professional, like she always undressed beautiful women for their bath. It wasn't easy.

With a haughty smile Bess stepped into the tub before giving another order.

"Put my clothes back in my bedroom. Bring me a nightie and a towel."

Cheryl moved as quickly as she could. When she came back into the room Bess was casually soaping up her breasts.

"Now then girl, you are to stand with the towel at the ready to dry me off when I finish. I'll tell you when I'm done."

Bess wanted to see just how much of a sissy girl Cheryl really was. So she had the sissy stand at attention, eyes lowered, while Bess relaxed and soaked in the tub. Bess took her time, teasing the sissy with every movement.

Once she felt that Cheryl had passed her test, she motioned the maid over to wash her hair for her. Cheryl complied, being very careful to apply just the right amount of shampoo, lathering it up, and then gently rinsing.

Once her hair was washed, Bess told the maid that she was finished with her bath. Cheryl held out the towel between them just like she always did for Lady Mildred. Bess appreciated the kind act of modesty. Clearly the sissy could control her vulgar impulses.

Cheryl helped Bess into her panties and nightgown. Then Bess instructed the maid to clean up the tub. While the maid started with that, Bess walked back to her bedroom.

Bess found the whole experience to be satisfying and sinfully erotic. She had teased the sissy girl and she had fun doing it. She found it to be a turn on to boss a maid around just like her employers always did with her.

When Cheryl finally returned to her own room she began to undress. When she stripped down to her panties she was surprised to find that even though she had not had an erection, she had soaked them with precum.

She changed her panties, put on a nightgown, and went off to bed.

Chapter 67. Vitamins

It had been months since Florence had introduced Cheryl to her special vitamins. One morning Cheryl went to Florence to tell her that she didn't feel right. She blushed when she said that she was unable to become erect and that maybe she should see a doctor.

Florence had been expecting just such a conversation. She pulled a bottle of pills out from her desk.

"Take one of these now dear, and another in the morning. If you aren't feeling any better tomorrow then I'll take you to see Doctor Carter."

Cheryl quickly swallowed one of the pills.

"Now off with you girl. You have work to do."

Cheryl went out of Florence's office to go back to her chores. Florence grinned at what she had accomplished.

She could already see the physical changes in Cheryl. She could tell by her softened skin that the hormones were taking effect. The stupid sissy girl probably already had a hint of breast growth too. It would be a longer process, but soon the sissy would have real breasts and perky nipples to go with them. She had shared that she couldn't get erect, so that was proof positive that Cheryl was well on her way to becoming her new self.

Some sissy girls find that once they are on hormone therapy that they've had their last erection. Florence smiled to herself at the thought. Braxton wanted Robin to be safe, and there was no doubt that she was now safe from the sissy girl.

Florence felt no sense of guilt. Quite the contrary. Cheryl had come into the mansion pretending to be a female. All Florence was doing was making sure that a female was what she was going to become. It was poetic justice.

Little by little Florence had seen the maid changing, becoming more and more feminine. The first time that the maid had helped to dress her she could feel her eyes all over her. These days, the maid went about her more intimate duties in the same manner that any domestic woman might.

She even had the maid powdering and perfuming her body after her bath. Such a luxury! Cheryl was such a sissy that she hadn't ever said a thing about having to powder the bottom of her supervisor.

Florence did enjoy the attention. A house manager should have a maid servant to help her dress and undress, shouldn't she? It had been her own idea. Lady Mildred was probably still thinking that Cheryl was her own private maid. That was hardly the case.

She laughed at the thought.

Chapter 68. Dinner and Dessert

That night Braxton invited his business partner, Trevor Tolworth, to dinner and to stay the night. Braxton had no idea that Trevor had met Robin and Cheryl before. He did know that Trevor was quite the lady's man. Braxton's plan for the night was simple enough. He wanted to let Trevor see the new maid and then take advantage of her. Florence had said that the sissy was coming along quite nicely. So it was to be a test for the maid to see just how much of a woman that she had become.

When he arrived, Trevor followed Bess to the dining room. He immediately recognized both Robin and Cheryl. However, he knew better than to say anything. Instead, he simply sat down for dinner with Braxton, Lady Mildred, and Robin.

At one point after dinner, Robin brushed by him and whispered in his ear.

"You have a lot of nerve coming here."

He grinned. She hadn't said anything to Braxton so he was safe. His partner wouldn't want to know that he had hit on his woman. It was okay that she still spurned him. He didn't want Robin anyway. At least not tonight. She still had her charms, so perhaps another night, but not this night. Braxton could bed the bitch for all he cared. He wanted the maid. He wanted Cheryl.

Bess was ordered to the kitchen while Cheryl stood at attention in the dining room while the guests conversed.

Braxton wanted to make sure that Trevor had a good look at Cheryl. He knew that those shapely legs and that ample bosom would be far too tempting for Trevor. Occasionally the maid was ordered to fill wine glasses. Trevor ravenously eyed her when she bent over slightly to pour.

Trevor kept careful watch on the captivating girl. He mentally undressed her several times during the evening. He remembered how good she was with oral servitude. He was hungry for her. He had never wanted a girl as much as he wanted that maid.

They sat and they talked well into the evening. It wasn't until it was very late that Braxton said it was about time to turn in for the night. Braxton gave a smile.

"Let's call it an evening. Trevor, I'll have the maid see you to your room. Good night."

Cheryl couldn't believe it. Braxton had ordered her to show Trevor to his bedroom! She didn't want to be alone with Trevor for even a second, particularly in his bedroom. She knew quite well what Trevor would do if left alone with her. She tried to ignore him while he followed her up the staircase to the bedrooms. She knew that he was looking up her dress but there wasn't a thing that she could do about it.

When they arrived in his bedroom, things happened quickly. Trevor took Cheryl by the hand and forced her down to her knees. Then he sat on the bed and stripped his pants off. After that he pulled her face to his cock and ordered her to pleasure him.

By this time Cheryl had become a rather compliant submissive. She had been shy enough before, but now the pills had changed her into a timid servant. She had no will to resist any person of authority. So she willingly took his cock in her mouth and slowly teased him with her tongue. Trevor encouraged her attentions by saying that she was a good bitch who certainly knew how to pleasure a man.

By this time Cheryl had enough practice that she had become proficient at cock sucking. Trevor moaned in ecstasy while she slowly picked up the pace. She could taste his precum dribbling into her mouth. Cheryl knew what was next.

Her first instinct was to back away, but she couldn't. He held her head with both hands while she finished him off. Then in a frantic thrusting motion, he pumped her mouth full of cum.

She had no choice but to swallow every last drop.

The wine and the sex took its toll. Trevor immediately passed out. Cheryl took what little dignity she had left and returned to her servant's quarters.

There, she looked at herself in the mirror. Her lipstick was smeared. He had mussed her hair. She felt like a cheap slut. She had given Trevor oral sex again and she hadn't even tried to resist him. He had insisted, and she had obeyed him.

She hadn't been able to summon the willpower to do much about it.

Chapter 69. Doctor Elizabeth Carter

Cheryl was relieved to be in Doctor Carter's office. She hadn't felt right for quite some time and she wanted answers. She had been even more woozy since Florence had given her additional pills the day before. She felt like she was floating on air, with her mind off in a different world. Florence had brought her into the clinic and the Mistress sat next to the exam table where Cheryl was positioned. Doctor Carter entered the room smiling.

"Hello Cheryl, I'm Doctor Elizabeth Carter. I see from your chart that you've done all of the preliminaries. You've completed your psychological evaluation, you've been living like a woman for quite some time, and you've been doing your hormone therapy. Very good for you.

I'll be doing your pre-op exam today and then we'll start your first surgery tomorrow. Right now I'd like to do a full exam. Before I have you change, tell me about your progress with the hormones. Have your nipples become more sensitive?"

Cheryl was in somewhat of a groggy daze but she managed to respond with a far-off voice.

"Yes, they've become very sensitive. I can't seem to keep my hands off of them. But I can't get an erection."

Doctor Carter smiled and made a notation on the tablet she was carrying.

"Very good. That's to be expected. Things are working right. That tells me that you've responded to the hormone therapy."

Suddenly Cheryl realized what the doctor had said. She yawned before she spoke in a tone that was half asleep.

"Surgery? Did you say *surgery*?"

Doctor Carter looked concerned. She glanced over at Florence. Florence gave her a little smile.

"I gave her a sedative so that she wouldn't worry so much. If you give us a minute I can talk with Cheryl and straighten things out."

"Very good. I'll be back in a minute."

Doctor Carter left Florence alone with Cheryl. Florence immediately began an explanation.

"Cheryl, I didn't want to tell you this, but I think that I should. Robin told me that she would much rather prefer a female maid and that she was going to send you away. I convinced her to keep you on staff. She agreed, but only on the condition that you go through a sex change operation. So I've been giving you female hormones to prepare you for your transition."

Cheryl stared straight ahead, still sleepy and in a state of confusion from the sedative. Finally she spoke slowly, in measured words.

"Robin wants me to…I'll do *anything* for Robin."

Florence grinned.

"Yes, that's right. *Anything* for Robin. Then you're okay with the surgery?"

"Yes, for Robin."

Doctor Carter came back into the room.

"Is everything okay then?"

Cheryl slowly nodded her head. Doctor Carter smiled.

"Very well. I need you to disrobe and put on the examination gown. Then up on the table and put your feet into the stirrups. I'll be back in a few minutes."

Doctor Carter motioned to Florence. They both left the room together. Out in the hallway Doctor Carter smiled.

"I've seen it before. There's no reason to worry. There's always trepidation when the time comes. That's one reason we do things in private, unlike other clinics. We don't want anyone judging until they see our finished product. Trust me, when she leaves here she'll be a whole new woman. I see here that Brittingham House has prepaid everything. Very good. Sign her in at the front desk and we'll give you a call in a few months when everything is complete."

"Thank you Doctor Carter. I'll leave her in your capable hands."

Chapter 70. Marry Me

It was the perfect moment. Dinner had finished and Robin and Braxton had walked outside into the lush flower garden. The water fountain provided the backdrop when Braxton dropped to his knees in front of her and took a ring out of his pocket.

"Robin you must marry me. I can't live without you."

Robin smiled.

"Must I?"

"Yes, you *must*. I love you like no other. Please, I beg you, marry me."

Robin looked at the ring. It was quite impressive. Braxton could easily afford the very best. She knew that should she marry Braxton that she would have a wonderful life. She would control him, and she would control his fortune. What a fortune it was! She would be shopping at Louis Vuitton and Prada instead of Macy's and Nordstrom. She would never set foot inside a Walmart *ever* again. A girl could become accustomed to that. At home, she would be pampered like a Queen. With the maids at her beck and call, she would never have to do a moment of housework. It would be sheer bliss.

How could any woman possibly turn all of that down? She pondered his offer.

"I would have conditions if I were to accept."

"Anything that you want dearest."

She gave him a devious grin. Florence had clearly made an impression on her.

"Anything? Well then, I think that I would take you…"

"Yes! I knew you would say yes!"

She shook her head.

"Not so fast. I would take you not as an equal, but as my slave. You would be my *sex* slave. You would adore and serve me like your Queen. I would control all of your finances and you would obey me in all matters."

He grinned.

"Does that include the bedroom?"

"*Especially* in the bedroom."

He took a deep breath.

"Okay, I agree."

She smiled.

"Really? Perhaps you should hear the rest. Did I mention that there would be no intercourse? At least not for you. I am a virgin and I intend to stay that way."

"But…"

"Those are my terms. Take them or leave them."

She knew that a submissive like Braxton couldn't possibly

turn down such an offer. Now that she knew the truth about Braxton she could control him just like Florence had done. She was right. He lowered his gaze to the floor.

"Okay. I agree."

Robin smiled. She had won.

Of course Braxton thought that she would eventually change her mind. Sooner or later, he thought, he would have Robin. It was only a matter of time.

Chapter 71. Chastity

Months had gone by since Cheryl had been sent to the clinic. He felt good about what he had arranged to be done with the maid. He couldn't very well live in a house where one of the maids could act on feelings she had for his wife.

Now that Robin had agreed to be married, there was only one more problem for Braxton to take care of. Robin brought the maid up, so it was time to put the rest of his plan into action.

"I was wondering Braxton, have you any idea what became of Cheryl? I've noticed that she hasn't been around. I do think that should be settled before our marriage. The thing is Braxton, if I marry you, what is to become of Cheryl?"

Braxton was ready for the question.

"Oh, I thought that you knew. Cheryl left us months ago. She didn't want to be a maid any longer. We'll need a replacement maid dear. I will have Florence see to it. This place can always use another maid. The more that we have, the better."

"That's not what I meant. She has feelings for me."

Braxton knew precisely what she meant. But he wanted her to think that Cheryl was no longer attracted to her.

"I believe that Cheryl found somebody else. Florence told me that she had left with another woman. I feel so bad for you honey. But I've already filed papers to annul your marriage so you are free to marry me.

Perhaps it is all for the better. Keeping Cheryl on staff would have been uncomfortable for me. Honey, you do realize that I couldn't have a sissy maid around the house who has designs on my wife. Yes, it's all for the better, don't you agree?"

Robin smiled. Braxton was right.

"I suppose you're right. It's best for all concerned."

Braxton leaned in and gave Robin a kiss.

"Yes, I want you all to myself. I'm sure that she has found someone else and she'll be happy too."

Robin kissed him back. His hands began to roam in places that made Robin feel so good. She made no attempt to stop him.

Once she was feeling loved, she spoke up.

"About our marriage relationship. I never did allow Cheryl to have me. She was such a sissy. She was essentially neutered by choice in her chastity. I do expect something similar from you. I think that you should wear a penis chastity and that I should hold the key."

"But I…"

"You thought that you would be able to make love to me? I don't think so. That's not the bargain we made. You'll service me with your tongue, but never with that cock of yours. Heaven only knows where *that's* been. I'll put an end to your fucking every girl in sight first thing. Any complaints? We can always call the marriage off right now."

He looked in her eyes, then he diverted his gaze. He could tell that she was serious.

"No Mistress. No complaints."

"I didn't think so."

"Oh, and you're to wear a slave collar. One that says "Property of Robin Dearing."

"Even to work?"

"*Especially* to work!"

Chapter 72. Unveiling

Almost a year had passed since Cheryl had been left at the clinic. It was time for the big unveiling. Florence had returned to the clinic where she had dropped Cheryl off. She was in a conference room meeting with the discharge specialist, one Suzanne Porter. Suzanne was giving her the scoop on Cheryl.

"First, we always encourage our clients to start anew. You know, a better body, a new life, and a new name to go with it. So Cheryl Meeks is now Cheryl Lovelace. She picked her name out herself. We have filed all of the legal papers and provided her with sufficient identification.

Naturally, there are many follow-up visits necessary for Cheryl. We can schedule those at your convenience.

We stressed to Cheryl that in order to best utilize her new image she should not ever refer to her old persona. She understands that she is never to divulge that she was once Cheryl Meeks. That always works best for our clients. Don't you think?"

Florence smiled. She already liked what she was hearing. Everything had proceeded just like it had been advertised.

"Cheryl came thru her sex reassignment surgeries with no problem at all. Doctor Carter was able to do everything that Cheryl wanted."

Florence suppressed a giggle. She had filled out the pre-op checklist herself. Cheryl actually had nothing whatsoever to do with it. Cheryl hadn't even seen it! Florence was finally going to supervise the maid that she always wanted. Cheryl would look and act like a demure little maid. She would have the girl worship her body. Naturally, a chastity belt would be in order. She would tease and deny her any orgasmic bliss whatsoever. The maid would live with unsatisfied lust. She would be so easy to dominate. Perfect!

Suzanne looked down at a post-op checklist. She casually read off the list.

"Yes, here it is. She was rather feminine to begin with so it was a pleasure for Doctor Carter to work with her. Mostly just minor touch-up work. She now has enhanced breasts, D cup, of course. She should know that the hormones might fill her out a bit more. She'll ultimately fill out to DD, I'm sure. She has a realistic vagina, wider hips and buttocks, desirable lips, and a pug nose. We modified her cheek bones. Just a touch to the vocal chords. She didn't need much there. She has a pleasant, distinctly feminine, voice."

Suzanne took a moment to take in the full impact of the work that Doctor Carter had accomplished. She was impressed.

"Wow, she really had the full treatment. We don't typically do that much work on one girl. Our dietician slimmed her down so she has a tiny little waist. She even received laser hair removal in all of the right places. Our stylist also spent time with her on makeup tips.

We heard that she works as a maid at The Aterberry. So the stylist thought that she would look better with black hair. That seems to look good on maids. So she dyed her hair black. We even brought a company in that provides maids for the wealthy. They put her through their intense training program. You know, making beds, cleaning toilets, lady's maid services, the full treatment. Her demeanor is perfect.

Her performance satisfactory. She'll fit right in with the rest of the maids at The Aterberry.

They even worked on her smile. The poor thing was so serious-minded that she never smiled. Can you imagine that? Maids should always smile happily when they go about their day, don't you think? Cheryl has a beautiful smile so they taught her to be sure to always smile while she works in order to show her enjoyment of servitude.

We also had our sex therapist work at length with her. They helped her with her daily vaginal ritual. There is a certain amount of required care, including keeping things stretched out properly.

We all noticed that she seemed to be sexually interested in women. The therapist said it was nothing to be concerned with. We don't see that very often in our clients so we felt it was just our imagination. All of the ladies who worked with her found her to be very cooperative. She is extremely sexually submissive. She's timid, obedient, and servile. Those are all good characteristics for a new young woman like her to have.

There was one thing. She was a bit troubled at first. It was almost like she was surprised with her surgery. That displaced feeling is not unusual for our new girls. You know, they sometimes get a bit of buyer's remorse when they find out that they're missing a little something they've always had."

Suzanne hushed a tiny little giggle.

"Snip, snip, snip. Once Doctor Carter finishes with a patient, there is no going back. Like it or not, Cheryl is a girl now. There's no changing that."

She suppressed a giggle at her own joke.

"Pardon me, a little bit of transgender humor there. Sometimes we can't help ourselves. One thing is for sure. She's quite a looker. She won't have any trouble at all finding male companionship. She did keep talking about a young man named Robin. I'm just curious. Is that the reason she wanted her sex reassignment surgery?"

Florence smiled. They thought that Robin was a guy!

"Yes, that was it. Robin. It was all about Robin."

"Well, I'm sure that Robin will be very happy with her. I think that he'll find her to be a very attractive young woman. Very suitable for Robin and for serving at The Aterberry. They're dressing her for discharge right now. She'll be here in a minute. If you sign this release, I can discharge her into your care."

Suzanne slid paper and pen over to Florence. Florence had to know.

"I'm just curious. Can Cheryl still have sex and if so, how will it feel for her?"

Suzanne smiled.

"We've had great success with that. During surgery, her feminine vagina was essentially fashioned from scratch. She has everything she needs to be a fully functioning young woman. Of course, she can't get pregnant. Just the fun stuff.

Doctor Carter does a most wonderful job with her patients. Cheryl has a pretty vagina and a real clitoris. The nerves from the tip of her penis became her clitoris so she gets the full experience. I personally wouldn't know, but they tell me that for new girls their orgasms are absolutely mind-blowing. They slowly build up until they positively explode with pleasure.

Cheryl will feel her orgasms all over her body more similar to that of a real girl than what she was previously accustomed to. It will be a whole new experience for her. You're a woman, you know what I'm talking about.

It will take her a while to become accustomed to her new body, especially her vagina. That's normal for our girls. She essentially has a whole new body, complete with vagina, clitoris, and boobs, unlike what she had before. When she looks in the mirror it will seem strange to her for a while to see the pretty girl staring back at her.

In the bedroom, she'll need to slowly work up to her orgasms the way that we do. You know, getting into the right headspace with the right guy. She may also need to lubricate with an oil before sex. Some do, some don't. Regardless, any guy having sex with her will have no idea that she is anything but the real deal—guys can't tell the difference."

Just when Florence finished signing, the conference door swung open and Cheryl Lovelace timidly stepped in.

Florence could hardly believe her eyes. The transformation had been absolutely incredible. Cheryl Lovelace looked like an entirely different person, completely unrecognizable as Cheryl Meeks. She was wearing a gold sweater dress that accentuated her new curves. Her full breasts proudly stood out. Her hips appeared extremely womanly. Mid height gold strappy heels adorned her feet. Her black hair flowed to her shoulders. She was expertly made up with glossy plump pink lips, matching blush, and bedroom eyes. Her new little pug nose gave her face an innocent girlish touch that belied the rest of her sexy appearance.

Not only was Cheryl wearing rhinestone earrings that dangled enticingly, she was still wearing her *slave* necklace and her *slut* ankle bracelet. They were the only visible remnants of Cheryl Meeks. She was a perfect vision of feminine sexual submission. Florence became aware of the musky sensual fragrance that came into the room with the girl. A suitable scent for a girl who appeared eager and ready for the bedroom.

The truth was that Cheryl was a knockout. She looked like a willing tart just begging for sex. Nobody would ever guess that Cheryl Lovelace had been Cheryl Meeks. No way! Cheryl Meeks had been a cute, innocent looking thing. Cheryl Lovelace appeared to be anything but innocent. Florence smiled. She had no intention of sending Cheryl to The Aterberry. She wanted to completely humiliate the sissy by having her work at Brittingham House right under Braxton's nose. He would have no idea!

She was sure that Braxton would be quite pleased with the new maid. Cheryl Lovelace was ripe for a good fucking. She was sure that sooner or later Braxton would get into her panties. She would be another in a long list of his conquests. She was sure that Braxton would fuck her brains out the first chance he got.

Robin would have no idea who the new maid was either. She would be none the wiser. So close and yet so far for Cheryl Lovelace. Perfect!

Cheryl would become Florence's new toy. She could tease and deny her to her heart's content. It would be delicious fun to have the maid at her beck and call. All the while the maid would long for sex in a manner like she could no longer have. Florence wanted to giggle at the delectable thought. But she managed to control herself. There would be plenty of time for such amusement later.

From this point on, the remainder of the plan would be easy to accomplish. Florence would bring Cheryl back to Brittingham House and she would become the new maid that Braxton had promised Robin.

On the way back to the mansion Mistress Florence spoke firmly to the new maid.

"You must never, *ever*, tell anyone who you really are. If I so much as suspect you have spoken, you'll get the paddling of a lifetime. Then I'll see that you're put out into the street without a stitch of clothing. Do you understand me girl?"

A timid little voice replied.

"Yes Mistress."

Chapter 73. Mirror Image

When Florence brought Cheryl back to Brittingham House she was introduced to Master Braxton, Mistress Robin and Lady Mildred as the new maid. Other than Braxton leering hungrily at the girl, they hardly paid any attention to the girl. Why would they? Robin only glanced at the girl for a moment. After all, a maid is a maid. There was not an inkling of recognition. They were clueless.

Florence put Cheryl Lovelace up in Cheryl Meek's old room so that she would feel at home. Florence had made a few modifications to tease the maid even further. She had replaced the maid's bra and panties. Cheryl would be wearing lace thong panties every day. The new shelf bras would plump her cleavage up even more than it already was. That way they would show prominently in the low-cut uniforms that Florence had provided for Bess and previously for Cheryl. The attire would drive Braxton crazy with lust and would remind Cheryl that she was a slutty maid.

Cheryl entered the room and slowly changed her clothes. She was a maid again and she would have to dress the part. She even put on the thong panties, shelf bra, and back-seamed stockings before she put on her new maid uniform.

Then she sat down at the dressing table to check her makeup. She looked in the mirror at the strange young girl who was staring back at her. It was her first look at her new self in uniform. She hardly recognized the girl that she saw there.

Her own image caused a delightful flutter of arousal. She was a pretty young thing, the kind of girl she would have paid special attention to before. But now she was a girl herself.

She was a mere maid destined to spend her life in the employ of Braxton Brittingham of Brittingham House.

She felt her nipples harden underneath her bra. Why did she find being a maid to be so humiliating? Why did such humiliation excite her so much? She had no idea. She just found the thought of working like a common maid to be erotic. She had to come to terms with that. She always had.

She put her hands in her lap. They touched the tops of her stockings. She looked down at her feminine legs. There wasn't a hair on them, further reminding her of just how much she had been feminized. They were the legs of a girl, pretty stockinged legs that ended in a lovely pair of heels.

Cheryl Meeks was gone. Cheryl Lovelace had taken her place forever. Cheryl Lovelace had a pretty smile, long black hair, and breasts that any young girl would envy. Another wave of pleasure rippled through her body at the thought. She gasped at the new feeling that started down below and ended at the tips of her nipples. She had been put in her place and now there was no turning back. Not ever. The thought of what had happened was turning her on like never before. They had told her that she was submissive and that she would enjoy servitude immensely. They were right. She had no idea why.

Cheryl needed to report for work. She had arrived just in time for Robin's family to come by for dinner. She stood up and straightened her apron. She noticed that there was a new bottle of perfume on the dressing table. She gave herself a spritz.

Then she took a deep breath and headed downstairs.

Chapter 74. Guest Rooms

Louise, Kendra and Wilma were excited to meet Robin's fiancé. They had been wowed by the drive up to the huge mansion and now they were ringing the bell at the front door.

Cheryl had appeared downstairs just in time to get the door. She half expected a greeting from the ladies. Instead, there was not a hint of detection. How could there be? Robin had also heard the bell and made an entrance at the same time they came in. The ladies simply moved right by Cheryl and gave Robin a big hug.

After Robin introduced the guests to Braxton, the families gathered at the dinner table. Bess and Cheryl dutifully served the meal while everybody merrily conversed. It wasn't until dessert had been served and the maids were waiting at attention that talk swung to the guests and their living arrangements. Robin started the conversation.

"Mom, the mansion is very big. We have several extra guest rooms. Would you be interested in moving in with us?"

That immediately got Braxton's attention. He had been looking out of the corner of his eye at Kendra and Wilma and he absolutely liked what he saw. He jumped in on the conversation.

"Yes, please! We would be happy to have you here!"

Cheryl heard the discussion and she wasn't so sure it was a good idea. Three more women would mean more work for her. She could still remember the spanking that Louise had previously given her. Plus, because of Kendra she had worn the faux vagina, and because of Wilma she had the *Slave* and *Slut* jewelry that she was still wearing. All in all, it was not a very appealing notion to have the ladies move in.

Not that anybody asked her, but regardless of Cheryl's feelings, Louise accepted the invitation. It was agreed. All three women would move into the mansion the very next day. Robin and Braxton were both elated. Lady Mildred was indifferent.

Braxton had no idea how dominant the ladies really were.

Chapter 75. Wedding

The wedding was held at Dearing House—the new name for the mansion previously called Brittingham House. Robin had seen to it that the sign at the gate was changed before the ceremony.

The minister was a woman named Madam Beatrice. She had presided over many such weddings so she was familiar with the unusual proceedings that were about to occur.

Lady Mildred was already seated. So were Louise, Kendra and Wilma. Also present was Braxton's assistant, Denise Hodge along with several other women from work. Chef Lolita was observing from the back of the room.

Bess and Cheryl were tending to Robin. They were checking everything for the last time to make sure that Robin looked perfect. The bride wore a beautifully fitted white gown. Her gown had a side slit that showed her left leg, exquisitely displayed in white stilettos. She had flowers in her flowing hair. She was a picture-perfect bride.

Florence was busy getting Braxton prepared. Robin had insisted that Braxton be properly humiliated so that he would know his place. It was a job that Florence relished.

He had succumbed readily to the basics though he had at first protested his enema. A taste of a bar of soap in his mouth put an end to any further complaints.

She had already completely shaved him. Other than his pencil thin eyebrows and his new long lashes, there was not a hair left on him. She had already put his penis chastity on him to secure his lust. He was so turned on by the humiliation that she had struggled to fit him in the chastity. But she had managed.

His legs looked womanly in white stockings held up by a frilly lace garter belt that framed his bare bottom. The garment left his penis, restrained in its chastity cage, fully exposed. His bottom was also open to whomever might care to take a glance. His strappy heeled sandals assured his firm rounded buttocks would be properly presented.

Florence had decided that a brassiere would be in order. So his fake breasts were safely secured in a strict cone bra that gave him pointed boobs.

Florence was busy seeing to his Turin collar. It was a metal ring with a nameplate in the front. The collar locked in place with an Allen Wrench. Florence sealed it closed with a touch of glue. The nameplate pronounced him to be *Property of Robin Dearing*. Just under the name was a small ring that Florence had attached a leather leash to.

The final touches would be makeup and a feminine wig. Flowing curls would touch his shoulders. A foundation, ruby red lips, blush, and smokey bedroom eyes completed his look. For a male who had been accustomed to being the Master of the house, it was complete degradation. After all, that had been the point. He found himself totally aroused at the transformation.

Florence had given him pills to calm him down. He found himself floating in sexual bliss at the humiliation. At the same time, he feared who might see him in such attire. He had spent his entire lifetime hiding his submissiveness from women. Now he would be exposed for what he really was.

In the other room, at the appropriate time, Bess gave Robin the leather riding crop that she was to carry during the ceremony. Then Cheryl and Bess accompanied Robin to the main dining hall were everyone was assembled.

Only then did Florence lead Braxton, by the leash, out to stand next to his bride. While the rest of the ceremony was somewhat traditional, based on the attire of the groom, the marriage was most certainly not going to be.

When prompted, Robin presented Braxton with a gaudy wedding ring. It was a woman's ring, the very ring that he had bought for Robin, meant to display him as spoken for. Braxton presented Robin with the key to his chastity.

The ceremony concluded, not with kissing the bride, but with the bride swishing her crop across Braxton's bare bottom. The motion made Braxton jump, and it left a red welt that rose across his buttocks. With that, all of the ladies in attendance applauded their approval of the proceedings.

There was no doubt whatsoever who was in charge in this new marriage.

Chapter 76. Reception

Chef Lolita really outdid herself with dinner. The ladies all sat in the dining room to enjoy the feast. There was room for all of the ladies at the table, but Braxton had to stand behind Robin. She held his leash during the meal while the maids served.

From time to time she turned to Braxton and fed him a bite. Robin drew a laugh from all the ladies when she quipped that Braxton was watching his figure so he wasn't eating much.

The chatter of feminine voices filled the room while Braxton was relegated to a lesser role. He simply stood and watched while the ladies conversed. His eyes roamed the room. He found the ladies to be exceptionally alluring in their fine attire. They seemed to be deliberately teasing him with short, tight, low-cut dresses. He found his cock repeatedly inflating until it pinched against his chastity before shrinking back down. It repeated the process over and over again. Essentially, Braxton was giving himself a mini fuck tease without hope of orgasm. His penis dripped precum in expectation of a climax that would never happen.

Near the end of dessert Lady Mildred noticed Braxton eyeing Cheryl. She had previously approved wholeheartedly of the marriage, exclaiming that Braxton had finally met a woman who could control him.

"Oh look Robin, your guy is already ogling another woman! Perhaps you should teach him a lesson!"

Robin, quite naturally, was disappointed.

"After we finish our meal I'll see to him."

After the dessert dishes were cleared Robin called Cheryl over. She handed her Braxton's leash.

"Take him to Florence. Tell her to fit the penis gag on him and then bring him back."

"Yes Mistress."

Florence was back in the kitchen supervising, so Braxton was led away by the pretty maid. When she returned, Braxton was gagged and his hands were secured to his metal collar with leather wrist cuffs.

The ladies ignored him. Now Cheryl held his leash while dinner conversation concluded. Finally Robin decided it was time to teach Braxton his lesson.

Robin had Cheryl lead Braxton by the leash over her lap. Then she told Bess to fetch her paddle. Braxton stayed over Robin's lap with his upturned bare bottom exposed until Bess returned.

The ladies laughed when the paddle landed squarely on Braxton's bottom. Then they clapped in rhythm with the paddle while Robin turned Braxton's bottom a stinging crimson color.

When Robin finished, she offered the other ladies a turn. They each took Braxton, one at a time, over their knees and spanked him like an adolescent child. Robin even had Cheryl take a turn, explaining that it was the best way to have Braxton keep his eyes to himself.

Chapter 77. Bridal Suite

The dinner guests had all left. Braxton was still standing in the dining room where he had been instructed to wait. With his hands still secured to his collar, he was unable to rub away the stinging sensation on his bottom. The ladies had been ruthless. Gagged, he was unable to protest his treatment. He had been paddled by each and every one of them, including the ladies from work and the maids. He would never be able to look them in the eye again.

Upstairs in the main bedroom, Bess and Cheryl were tending to Robin. They had carefully undressed her by glow of candlelight, and now she was reclining on her big brass bed. She gave the maids instructions on how to bring her sex slave to her chambers and then she sent them off.

Bess and Cheryl giggled when they arrived back at the dining room where Braxton still waited. Bess pulled on a pair of latex gloves while she spoke.

"Mistress Robin says that she will not be using her dildo harness tonight, so you are to be plugged. Bend over *slut*."

She emphasized that last word. She had long waited to put the arrogant Braxton in his place. She would no longer have to ever give him any respect whatsoever. It felt wonderful for her.

Braxton felt the pinch of his chastity. The *maid* had *ordered* him to bend over like he was some kind of slave! Such exquisite humiliation was almost too much for him. His encased cock freely oozed precum that dribbled down his legs moistening his stockings.

He stayed bent over in position while Bess lubed up his bottom. Her fingers probed deep inside. Not so much because he needed to be lubed that deep, but more because she just wanted to humiliate him. Then, in one quick thrust, Bess shoved a butt plug up his ass that caused him to gasp in arousal beneath his penis gag. Both maids laughed at his hilarious predicament while Cheryl led him by the leash to Mistress Robin's bedroom. His bottom wiggled while he walked. Between his heels and his butt plug, he had no choice but to give a feminine swish.

Robin ordered her slave to his knees. Then she dismissed the maids before commanding him to pleasure her.

He buried his face deep in her love nest. He licked and lapped away, driving her to exquisite sexual heights. His tongue did its amazing magic on her until she screamed in total ecstasy.

Sexually fulfilled and completely exhausted, she ordered her slave to sleep on the floor at the foot of her bed. He willingly complied.

Chapter 78. Supervision

Braxton had spent a full week in Robin's bedroom servicing her like a mere sex slave. Even when she went downstairs to eat, Braxton had remained in her chambers. Quite a few things had changed since the wedding day.

Florence had moved into the bedroom where Robin had previously stayed. Braxton's belongings had been removed and discarded.

Now it was time for Braxton to go back to work. He was to perform an embarrassing chore that he dreaded. The previous evening he had been moved to the servant's wing of the mansion, into one of the tiny bedrooms that the maids were assigned to. He had slept in a frilly nightgown that night. Since he had been naked all week, even wearing a woman's nightgown felt comforting. He hadn't slept very well though. The soft panties he wore and the lace nightgown had teased him all night long.

Now it was morning and Braxton was confused. There was nothing but female clothing in his room. Feminine lingerie and maid uniforms! Certainly they didn't expect him to go to work in a maid uniform, did they? Then there was the collar, and his fingernails were still polished to match the lipstick he had worn for his wedding. There had to be a mistake!

Still wearing his nightgown, he tiptoed over to Robin's bedroom and quietly opened the door. She was sound asleep. He knew better than to wake her. He decided to see Florence — she would know what he should do.

When he opened the door to the House Manager's bedroom,

he found Cheryl getting Mistress Florence dressed for the day. The room that he had previously occupied looked entirely different. Had he not been certain that the room next to Robin's had been his, he would have never recognized it. It had been re-painted, new lace curtains hung, and a new larger vanity covered with cosmetics was off to the side. The bed had been replaced with a big brass bed. Mistress Florence was clearly enjoying the attention of her maid. She hardly glanced at Braxton.

"See Maid Bess. She'll tend to you this morning. Go and report to her now."

Braxton was appalled. Even the House Manager didn't have time for him! He was to *report* to the pretty young maid for instruction. He couldn't believe what was happening. But he had no choice!

He quickly went back to the servant's wing and entered the bedroom where maid Bess slept. She had just dressed herself and was seated, busy brushing her hair at her vanity. He stood behind her while he talked. She looked at him in the mirror while she continued with her hair.

He almost choked on the words. Humiliation flushed his cheeks when he spoke.

"Miss Bess, Mistress Florence said that I was to report to you. I have to go…"

She interrupted him.

"Yes, yes. I know. You're to go to the company today and turn it over to Denise Hodge. One more day of work and you can be back to your domestic duties here. Why aren't you dressed? What's the problem?"

Braxton hardly knew what to say. Surely she didn't expect him to go to work dressed like a maid, did she? He barely mumbled out his problem.

"Miss Bess, there are only maid uniforms in my room. I can't very well go to work dressed like a maid, can I?"

There was no response from Bess. She was tempted to reply that she wore a maid uniform every day, so it was no big deal. But she already had a plan so she stayed silent. She was enjoying teasing him. Braxton continued, now sounding much more desperate.

"Miss Bess, my head has been shaved, all I have is a wig with long curls. I'll look silly. The girls at the office will laugh at me. Please!"

Having finished brushing her hair, Bess turned to face Braxton. She did feel a touch of pity for him because she knew how difficult the day would be for him. But Mistress Florence had given her instructions the previous evening. His fate was already sealed. She decided to have some fun with him anyway.

"Down on your knees and beg me. Then *perhaps* I'll help you out. I wouldn't want Braxton Brittingham to be humiliated on his last day on the job."

Chapter 79. Dressed For Success

Braxton couldn't believe what he had done. He had dropped to his knees and begged the maid for mercy. Yes, the *maid*! The same maid he had hired and subsequently repeatedly fucked. The same maid he had looked down upon as merely hired help.

Thankfully, she had agreed to help him out. Things hadn't quite worked out quite the way that he had hoped, but still it was better than going to work in a maid uniform. She had him return to his new bedroom and wait for her to return with a few articles of clothing.

Miss Bess had insisted that Braxton wear proper female underwear. Braxton agreed, thinking that nobody would see his underwear anyway. Miss Bess had rummaged in the armoire drawers for a matching bra and panty set, along with a garter belt and stockings. She insisted on padding out the bra with rolled up stockings. That's how he came to be wearing full lady's lingerie.

When he had tried to protest, she had said not to worry. She said that it would all be covered up. Indeed it was.

Miss Bess produced a sheer white nylon blouse and a pair of pull-on stretch pants. Braxton recognized the outfit immediately. These were Robin's hand-me-downs, the same attire she had worn right after Braxton realized that Robin was really a woman. Bess watched with a self-satisfied smile while Braxton slipped into them.

Braxton would not have to wear the curly wig to work.

Instead, Miss Bess provided him with another wig. This wig had long hair that was pulled back into a ponytail that hung in back almost to his waist. It was possible that it *might* be construed to be a male wig, but not very likely. Still it was better than girlish curls.

Miss Bess had Braxton sit at the vanity. She said that a touch of makeup was necessary to complete the picture. Braxton could see himself in the mirror. He certainly didn't look like a domestic maid, but he still appeared feminine. He could see the outline of his bra through the sheer blouse fabric. Together with the wig he still gave the impression that he was a woman.

Braxton wanted to protest while she carefully applied his makeup. But he found that he simply couldn't resist. He found the young maid taking charge of him like that to be sexually captivating. Once a submissive, always a submissive!

When she finished applying his lipstick he knew that he wouldn't be fooling anybody. He didn't move when she put a bracelet on his wrist. The necklace she put on him and the matching clip-on earrings didn't help either. He looked like a woman. But he guessed that since Denise and other women from work had been at the wedding that it most likely didn't matter anyway.

Maid Bess had him slip into a pair of heels, then spritzed him with perfume before pronouncing him ready to go to work. His eyes pleaded with the maid in a final attempt for mercy. Maid Bess grinned at her creation. She teased him.

"You look great honey. Have a nice day!"

Chapter 80. On The Job

Braxton felt silly sitting at his desk. It was his first day on the job after the wedding and it would be his last. He had a new nameplate on his desk pronouncing that he was now Braxton Dearing. He was wearing his collar inscribed with *Property of Robin Dearing*. He wore the gaudy wedding ring that Robin had given him, clearly a woman's ring. Underneath, he was wearing women's panties over his chastity encased cock. His hair was pulled back into a ponytail, a further visible telltale of how he had been dominated.

Braxton couldn't have been more embarrassed than he was that morning. Many of the staff had been at the wedding. Those who did not attend surely already knew everything. His secret adoration of women and the secret of his submissive nature were both common knowledge among the ladies.

How could he possibly ever be in charge again?   It didn't matter anyway. Robin had given him explicit instructions. He had to appoint his assistant to lead the company.

All of the ladies in the office giggled when they first saw him. There were a few audible gasps and snickers when they saw how the boss had been transformed. There was no question in their minds that he was dressed like a woman. Robin had clearly dominated him to the point of dressing him up like a female and sending him to the office.

How deliciously wonderful it was! They could see thru his blouse that he was wearing a bra. A woman's bra! It was padded out so that he obviously had a woman's bust. More snickers followed.

At first nobody said a word. If the boss wore female clothing to work, that was his choice. But the giggles quickly became louder. The ladies couldn't help themselves.

The women he had ogled for so long could now take revenge on him and they liked the idea. There would be no pity from them either. He couldn't have possibly been humiliated any further than he already was. Tech mogul Braxton Brittingham had come to work dressed like a woman!

But it was even worse than that. His assistant, the beautiful young girl named Denise, had spoken with his wife after the wedding ceremony. Robin had given the girl permission to spank Braxton on his bare bottom should he step out of line with any of the ladies at the office. Robin had also given her a wooden paddle to do the job with. Plus Robin had also presented her with a Humbler of her own, along with tips on how to use it.

The pretty young girl, dressed in a tight miniskirt that flaunted her legs, sat just outside his office with a big smile on her face. The wooden paddle was prominently displayed on her desk right next to the Humbler. With such a display so evident, she knew that she was the most powerful woman in the company.

The ladies teased Braxton unmercifully. They clearly no longer respected him and they weren't shy about showing it. When he asked a young female intern, named Tiffany, to do a mundane task, she giggled and then told him to do it himself. Then she stopped for a moment and demanded that he kiss her feet. Braxton couldn't help himself. He knelt at her feet and obediently kissed her heels while she laughed at his humiliation.

Once the other ladies saw that he had obeyed a mere intern they all wanted in on the fun. One of the ladies who Braxton had previously leered at before his marriage went into his office and slapped him across his face. Another went in and gave a playful tug on his steel collar before laughing at him.

The day descended into a female free-for all with the ladies teasing, tantalizing, and dominating the male who had previously been their supervisor. He seemingly no longer had any authority whatsoever over them.

The ladies erupted into complete raucous laughter when the pretty intern came back into his office and demanded that Braxton kiss her ass. Tiffany lifted her skirt and presented her bottom to him to be worshipped.

Again, he couldn't help himself. He simply could not refuse the orders of an authoritative woman. Certainly not dressed the way that he was. He knelt down behind her and he shamefully complied.

Chapter 81. Maid Duties

Meanwhile, back at Dearing House, Cheryl and Bess were busy cleaning up after the wedding. Louise, Kendra and Wilma had decided to stay so there were guest rooms to tend to. The maids were intently working away changing sheets.

Cheryl was happy to return to her full duties. She felt very comfortable with her new body doing domestic work. Her maid uniform fit her like a glove. She no longer had to hassle with breast forms but she could still fill out a D cup. Her thong panties touched her in sensitive places when she bent over, but she was becoming accustomed to it. The push up bra that showcased her breasts served to accentuate her breasts and make her feel even more feminine.

The change seemed miraculous to her. She hardly remembered her transformation. It was all something of a blur. Now her head was clear and she had her full attention on the task at hand.

Robin hadn't said a word to her. Cheryl reasoned that she was just keeping Cheryl's old persona a secret. It was fine with Cheryl. So long as she could be near Robin she was happy.

She had strange feelings. Doctor Carter had said that things would be different. She still had a feeling of arousal even though she no longer had anything to have an erection with. She still found feelings of submission to be erotic, though oddly, those feelings caused her nipples to tingle. She found herself touching her nipples at the end of the day because it felt so good to do so. Doctor Carter had been right. She did enjoy touching her nipples more than ever before.

Cheryl had even experienced mind-blowing orgasms. She found that if she touched her new clitoris just right after using her vibrator and teasing her nipples she could set off an orgasm that rippled thru her body. It was an incredible sensation, unlike anything that she had ever experienced before.

Cheryl realized that with Louise, Kendra, and Wilma all staying at the mansion that she would have more work to do than before. She would be quite busy with laundry. Hand washing lingerie for all of the women every day would be a big chore. But it was her job to do it, so she was pleased to see to it while Bess tended to other things.

Cheryl looked up from her work. She thought that she had heard Mistress Robin ring the servant's bell. She left Bess and quickly went down the stairs and then down the long hallway to the deck at the rear of the mansion where Mistress Robin was lounging out in the sun. She had moved as quickly as she could in her heels.

Mistress Robin was wearing her two-piece bikini and a pair of dark sunglasses. She was reclining with her feet up just taking in the morning. Cheryl tried to remain professional even though she wanted to gaze at length at the beautiful woman.

Cheryl gave a cute little curtsy.

"How may I be of service Mistress?"

Robin didn't even look at the maid. Without so much as glancing at the girl she placed her order.

"Fresh orange juice and toast. I'll take them here."

"Yes Mistress."

Cheryl curtsied and went off to fulfill Robin's request.

Just then Robin's cell rang. A video call was coming in from Braxton's assistant Denise. She touched answer to accept the video call.

Chapter 82. Down A Few Pegs

Robin couldn't believe what she was seeing. It was a live picture coming straight from Braxton's office. Braxton was bent over his desk, with his pants and his underwear pulled down. His red bottom had obviously been spanked.

His penis chastity was on the desk next to him. A young girl was taking his penis in her hand and she was pulling it back between his legs. She was wearing a tight mini-skirt, extremely high heels, and a nylon blouse that presented all of her charms in all of her feminine glory. Robin surmised that the pretty girl must have gotten Braxton into trouble. Dressed like she was it was no wonder Braxton was ogling her. Of course, that was just the behavior that Robin wanted him to be punished for.

Robin could hear several women in the background all talking and laughing at the same time so she knew that there were more witnesses in the room. Denise spoke.

"I'm teaching Braxton a lesson, just like you said that I could."

"I can see that. Good job. What happened?"

The young girl was fastening the Humbler on Braxton's penis while Denise continued. His cock was in place and she was tightening it up.

"Our young intern is Tiffany. That's her putting the Humbler on for Braxton right now. He was caught trying to look up her skirt. I saw it myself."

In fact Denise had seen Braxton obeying the intern when she

ordered him to kiss her ass. But it was of no matter. It was not like Braxton could appeal the sentence that Denise had decreed.

Robin could see the young intern finishing up with the Humbler. There was more feminine laughter. Braxton's balls were presented at just the right height while he was held in place bent over his desk. Now Tiffany had a plastic ruler in her hand and she was smacking Braxton's balls. Robin could hear him yelping with each swat.

Robin smiled.

"I'm glad you called Denise. Tell Braxton that what you do with him at the office is nothing compared to what he gets when he comes home."

Tiffany handed the ruler to another girl. With a big grin on her face, she took a whack at his balls. He flinched in obvious pain. There was feminine shrieking in glee at the amusing come-down that the boss was getting. Robin could hear more feminine voices asking for a turn with the ruler. Denise finished up the call.

"Just letting you know what's going on here. He's already written a memo resigning and promoting me to company president. Thank you Robin! I'll send him home when we're done with him."

"Thank *you* Denise. Thank all of the other ladies too. Make sure those balls remain blue!"

"Will do!"

Chapter 83. Trevor Tolworth Visits

Trevor had wanted to check with Braxton regarding the changes at the firm. Braxton didn't really want to meet with him. He had already been humiliated enough for the day. But Trevor had insisted, so he relented. He arranged for Trevor to come to dinner and stay the night so that they could talk at length.

Bess opened the door for Trevor and led him back to Braxton's home office. Trevor was a bit shocked at his business partner when he saw him. He shook his hand and stared at Braxton's attire. Braxton was still dressed like he had been for the office that morning. Trevor smiled.

"Married just a few days and pussy whipped already?"

Trevor pointed at Braxton's neck.

"That's quite a collar that you're wearing."

"It was from my wife. She has quite the sense of humor."

"Well, I can certainly see that."

They both laughed.

"Braxton, I'm here because I was told that we are both done with the company. An early retirement with recurring stipend, right?"

Braxton nodded.

"That's right. I think it best for both of us."

"Very well. I have other things to do."

They talked for an hour or so before Bess arrived and proclaimed that dinner was ready. They moved to the dining room where Lady Mildred and Robin were already seated waiting for them.

When Cheryl brought out the first course, Trevor couldn't believe his eyes. Where in the world did Braxton find these maids? The maid who opened the door was hot enough. This girl was eye-candy if ever there was such a thing. He felt his cock stiffen up in his lap. He quickly placed his cloth napkin over it to conceal his obvious lust for the girl.

The meal was slowly served and consumed. However, the meal did not quench Trevor's hunger for the new maid. Finally he just had to know her story. Cheryl was outside the room when he spoke.

"Braxton, what's the word on the new maid?"

Braxton wasn't expecting an inquiry. He should have known. The only guy who had bedded more women than Braxton was Trevor. He thought that it would be a neat prank on Cheryl to send Trevor her way. The new girl would have no idea that Trevor would most likely bed her. Even if Braxton couldn't have her, he could at least leave it to his business partner to sample her wares.

"She's Cheryl. She's quite unattached. Quite the looker isn't she?"

Trevor smiled.

"Would you mind terribly if I dipped a bit in the pond?"

"Of course not. Help yourself. She's all yours."

Trevor stood up.

"If that's the case, then I'll be calling it a night."

With that, he excused himself and headed towards the bedrooms. He met Cheryl in the hallway just outside the dining room. He took her by the hand and led her up the stairs towards his guest room.

There would be no denying him tonight!

Chapter 84. Humbled

Trevor was ready to pillage Cheryl's charms. He had mentally undressed her during dinner and now she really was naked and right there for the taking. Now that he had teased her nipples, she was so aroused he could see that she couldn't resist him. He was ready to take her.

He quickly stripped his clothes off. Cheryl didn't move. She simply stared in wide-eyed arousal while he prepared to impale her with his erect lust. He brushed her nipples one more time for extra encouragement. She moaned in sexual pleasure and spread her legs wide apart. Just when he was about to plunge cock first into her virgin love nest, the door to the bedroom opened up.

Trevor froze in position while Robin and Florence came right up to the bed. Robin spoke first.

"I see that nothing has changed with you Trevor. You are still the same person that you were before. You're a lout, a brute, and a scoundrel if ever there was such a thing. What a pig! Shame on you! You need to be taught a lesson."

She turned to the nude maid.

"Leave us Cheryl."

The maid quickly gathered her clothes and went out the door. Still naked, she hastily went down the hall to her bedroom so she could dress up again.

It's not like the ladies were expecting anything different from Trevor. They had come prepared. Florence had brought her paddle with her and Robin was holding a Humbler. Florence took Trevor by the hand and led him over to a chair by the dressing table. He was so shocked at their unwelcomed appearance that he made no effort to resist going over Florence's lap. She held one of his arms behind his back. Her leg was draped over one of his legs, pinning him in position.

Florence held nothing back. Robin had told her that Trevor needed to be taught who was sexually in charge, and it was certainly not him. She smacked away at his upraised bottom while he wriggled helplessly without results in a worthless attempt to free himself.

Florence punctuated each smack of the paddle with a verbal reprimand.

"You will be respectful to women!"

Smack!

"You will be obedient to all women!"

Smack!

"Women are your superiors!"

Smack!

"You are my bitch!"

Smack!

"You'll lick pussy on command!"

Smack!

On and on it went. After Florence had turned his bottom a deep shade of red, she let him up with the command to kneel in front of her. With his bottom stinging from the reprimand, Trevor quicky obeyed.

Then Robin came up behind him. She reached between his legs and in a quick movement the Humbler was in place. Robin laughed.

"He's all yours now Florence. I'll be back in an hour."

Trevor had never been treated like that by a woman before. He found the authoritative Florence to be an incredible turn-on. His bottom burned. He certainly didn't want her to spank him again. So he decided it was best to obey her.

When Robin returned she found Trevor still kneeling in front of Florence, penis still restrained by the Humbler. Now he was busy licking her toes. His bottom remained a deep red. He was wearing a Turin slave collar, just like the one that Braxton wore. Only his said *Property of Mistress Florence*. Florence had also taken a black marker and written *Florence's Bitch* on his red bottom.

Robin smiled.

"Indelible marker?"

"Of course!"

Florence looked down at the humbled slave at her feet.

"You may stop now bitch."

There was a tiny meek reply.

"Thank you goddess Florence. I enjoyed worshipping your feet."

Florence smiled.

"How do you greet goddess Robin?"

The meek voice continued.

"I'm so sorry for how I treated you goddess Robin. Please smack my balls so that I may learn my lesson."

The last words were a tiny little whisper.

Robin shrieked with approval.

"Well done Florence! Exactly what I wanted!"

With that she slapped and then squeezed Trevor's balls until he let out an excruciating yelp.

"Oh, did that hurt bitch? Maybe from now on you'll treat women better. You'll keep that thing of yours in your pants from now on, won't you?"

The timid voice submitted to her superiority.

"Yes goddess Robin."

Robin giggled.

"I love it Florence. He's *perfect*!"

Robin smiled.

"I think that he's ready to go now. Remove the Humbler and

put him in the chastity."

In minutes Trevor was free of the Humbler, but restrained in a metal penis chastity. Florence attached a leash to his collar and the two women led him downstairs to the front door. Trevor was speechless when Florence detached the leash and pushed him out the door — still naked.

Robin laughed.

"That was *fun!*"

Florence agreed.

"That was, but that's nothing compared to what he gets the next time we see him."

Both women laughed.

Chapter 85. Florence The Sadist

Florence had become a confirmed sadist who was always thinking of ways to dominate those around her. She had Braxton wrapped around her finger for quite some time. She always enjoyed taunting him and having him drool over her body. Then leaving him hot and horny without ever having his way with her.

She enjoyed dominating Bess too. The girl was a slut and she was easy to boss around. Bess had provided her with hours of oral sex so she knew exactly what was Bess's best attribute in the bedroom.

She was pleased with herself for turning Cheryl into a female servant, but she wanted to do more than that with the girl. So she came up with the idea of switching responsibilities between Bess and Cheryl.

Bess became Lady Mildred's personal maid while Cheryl became Robin's personal maid. Florence was delighted with the concept. In her mind she could imagine the toll such an arrangement would take on the neutered sissy girl. She knew that Robin had no interest in having sex with a woman. The sissy girl would be turned on by the experience of being so close to Robin, but with a vagina and no penis, the maid would be totally frustrated. What a grand idea!

Florence always enjoyed a tease and denial session and this would be the ultimate. She couldn't wait to get started. She called both maids into her office and then explained that the change was to take effect immediately.

While Bess wasn't particularly excited about tending to Lady Mildred again, Cheryl was excited about serving Mistress Robin. That is, she was excited until that evening when it came to seeing to her needs.

Cheryl hadn't realized that since the wedding Mistress Robin had moved to the larger master bedroom. Braxton had moved to the smaller room that Robin had previously occupied. While they weren't sleeping together, Robin had taken to having Braxton in her room in the evening before they went to bed.

Part of Cheryl's duties were to stay in the room in case she was needed. She was treated to the humiliation of standing at attention, eyes lowered, while Robin teased Braxton. They would make out on Robin's bed, tongues probing deep. Cheryl couldn't help but to become insanely jealous. Occasionally Cheryl would sneak a peek at the lewd activities.

That first evening, at one point, Cheryl had a clear view of Braxton's penis chastity. She was thankful that it hadn't been removed. She wanted Robin for herself. Then it occurred to her that she couldn't really give Robin what she wanted anymore. Now she was a simple female maid. She had been completely emasculated so she could no longer even dream of performing manly duties for Robin. It was frustrating indeed!

Cheryl could only take the frustration for a few days. Then she went to Florence and asked for the arrangements to be put back the way that they had been. Florence pretended to be reluctant, but she finally agreed.

It was only after Cheryl left her office and went back to work that Florence laughed to herself. It had been great fun teasing the maid like that!

Chapter 86. Florence At Heart

Florence was not heartless. She knew that Cheryl needed sexual satisfaction. The kind that of satisfaction that a girl can only get from a good sound fucking. That was where Trevor came in.

Since the day they had put Trevor in chastity, his cock had remained secured under lock and key. Florence thought that it would be amusing to have him get together with Cheryl for a little bit of a fuck-fest tease.

Robin, Braxton, and Mildred were all out of the house when Florence put her scheme into action. She told Cheryl that she was going to do her a favor and give her a *real* fucking. Then she told Cheryl to go up to her bedroom and wait naked on her bed for her lover to arrive.

Cheryl was so sexually starved that she obeyed without hesitation. Florence had invited Trevor over with the tease that she could arrange it so that he could have sex with Cheryl. Naturally, he couldn't get there fast enough.

Florence led Trevor up to Cheryl's bedroom where the maid was waiting naked on her bed. Florence sat down at the dressing table and put a paddle that she had carried along with her on the table.

Trevor's eyes widened when he saw the naked maid just waiting to be taken. But he had a problem. He was still wearing his penis chastity. He looked at Florence for sympathy. She smiled.

"In due time. You have to earn the honor first."

His cock was already straining in its prison, so he was ready to do *anything* to take the maid. Florence explained.

"First you have to warm up Cheryl. She needs a real man in her cunt, but she needs to be properly lubricated. I want you to strip, get down on your knees, and then I want you to pleasure Cheryl with your tongue."

Trevor couldn't move fast enough. In seconds he was naked and lapping away at Cheryl's pussy. Cheryl had never experienced oral servitude before, so her new female genitals responded immediately to his oral attention.

Florence watched stoically while Trevor brought Cheryl to a mind-blowing orgasm. Cheryl screamed in ecstasy when waves of pleasure finally rose from her clitoris, pulsed thru her body up to her hardened nipples, and then went rippling back down again all the way to her toes. Her whole body seemed to vibrate in sexual fulfillment. She had never experienced such rapture before. She passed out from the pleasure on the bed.

Trevor was satisfied that he had done his job. Now he was ready for his prize. Florence held the key to his chastity in front of him.

"One more thing Trevor. You need to prove that you're man enough for Cheryl. You're to come over my lap for a spanking. If you can endure the paddle without spurting then I'll let you have Cheryl. Agreed?"

Trevor was so excited that it didn't matter what Florence asked him to do, the answer was yes. Florence took the key and removed his penis chastity. His cock immediately enlarged into a lewd salute to her gorgeous femininity.

Florence gave it a casual stroke. The sarcasm dripped from her words.

"Oh, it has been *sooo* long baby. I'll bet you just *can't* wait!"

Trevor muttered something unintelligible before Florence raised her dress a bit giving him a good look at her legs. His eyes widened with lust. Then she took him over her lap before she casually picked up the paddle.

"Okay Trevor, show me what a *man* you are."

She slapped his bottom with the paddle. That caused him to buck and rub his hard-on against her stockings. She slapped him again, harder this time. He pressed his cock firmly against her stockings. Florence taunted him even more.

"You do want Cheryl, don't you dear? You want to give the maid a good fucking, don't you?"

It had been so long since Trevor had been able to have an erection that he couldn't help himself. It only took a few whacks with the paddle before he moaned in ecstasy and spurted his cum all over Florence's stockings. She laughed at his inability to control himself, then she let him stand back up.

He sheepishly looked down on her wet stockings like a little boy who had broken something valuable. Now she teased him.

"You naughty boy! I guess you won't be having Cheryl today. Such a shame. Look at this mess you made. Lick it up!"

She said it with such authority that he couldn't resist. He lapped every last drop up off of her stockings with his nose just inches away from her glorious womanhood. When he finally finished, his cock was shrunken to a worthless little stub. He looked to Florence for pity.

She gestured at his flaccid little cock. Then she taunted him with an amused tone.

"You couldn't do much with *that* anyway. Bring *it* here."

He reluctantly moved forward. Florence put his penis back in chastity, securing it safely with a click. Then she tucked the key in her bra between her breasts.

Trevor couldn't believe what had just happened. He had come so close to fucking the maid but he hadn't been allowed to. His bottom stung from the paddle. He could still see the tantalizing vision of Cheryl sleeping naked on the bed when he dressed himself back up.

Florence had completely humiliated him.

Chapter 87. Work Day

With all of the ladies staying at Brittingham House, there was so much laundry to do that Cheryl was flustered. With the large volume of clothing to be laundered distracting her, she mistakenly put Lady Mildred's corset in the washer along with a red sweater. When the cycle finished, Cheryl took the corset out of the washer and stared at it in horror. Now the white corset was a rosy shade of pink. It was an honest mistake, but one with significant consequences.

She decided to fess up to Lady Mildred what she had done. After showing Lady Mildred the garment, she stood at attention in front of her with her eyes lowered. Lady Mildred was hardly amused.

"Stupid girl! How could you do such a thing to my favorite corset!"

Lady Mildred was no stranger to sloppy maid service. She was also no stranger to disciplining a maid when careless service required it. She went straight to her dresser and pulled a large wooden paddle out of the bottom drawer.

"I'll teach you to pay attention to what you're doing! Lift that tawdry excuse for a dress you're wearing and lower your panties. That's it. Now bend over and touch your heels!"

Lady Mildred snapped the commands so fast that Cheryl complied without a thought. She felt silly holding the position while Lady Mildred continued to lecture her.

"I've noticed your slipshod work from the moment you arrived. I'll not have that careless attitude of yours in my home. I can see that you're more concerned with having your muff fluffed by Master Braxton than you are with your work. Such a brazen hussy!"

With that Lady Mildred let the paddle land with a loud smack squarely on the maid's behind. The force of the paddle almost caused the maid to tip over. Four more resounding cracks of the paddle followed. Lady Mildred paused for a moment to admire the rosy red that spread over the maid's bottom.

"I'll teach you to ruin my corset you fucking harlot!"

After ten more of Lady Mildred's best the maid's bottom was well warmed. Cheryl felt a sensation deep down unlike anything she had ever experienced before. Fuck! She was turned on by the spanking!

Lady Mildred ordered her to straighten up. Then she threw the corset at the maid.

"Put it on right now girl. You're to wear it every day from now on. Snap to it!"

The maid found the corset that fit the slightly built Lady Mildred so well to be tight on herself. She squeezed into it and after that Lady Mildred gave an extra tug on the strings. Cheryl found that the underbust corset lifted her breasts in a teasing manner while pulling her stomach tightly in at the same time. Lady Mildred was pleased with what she saw. She told the maid that she was through with her for the moment.

"Now put your dress back on, and off with you before I get really angry!"

The maid hurried off to tend to her duties.

Chapter 88. Conversation

Bess and Cheryl were clearing dishes from the table. Robin, Lady Mildred, Louise, Kendra and Wilma were savoring the delicious meal that chef Lolita had prepared. Louise smiled at Robin.

"That meal was awesome. Chef Lolita is really something."

Robin nodded.

"Yes, she is quite extraordinary."

Lady Mildred chimed in.

"Good help is so hard to find. Chef Lolita is a keeper. Not like that other maid who used to work here. What was her name?"

Robin answered her.

"Do you mean Cheryl Meeks?"

Lady Mildred nodded.

"That's right. Cheryl Meeks. What a Bimbo. She didn't know her corset from her knickers. I had to put her in a corset just so she could know what it was. The girl was clueless. What ever became of that girl anyway?"

Again Robin responded.

"I was told that she didn't want to be a maid any longer so she just ran off."

Lady Mildred gave a chuckle.

"No loss there. Better that she finds another occupation than pretend to be a maid. She was a dimwitted maid if ever there was one."

Bess cleared the last dessert dish from the table. Lady Mildred took a long look at the girl before voicing her disapproval.

"Tell me Robin, who picked out the uniforms for our current maids? They look like Parisienne Hookers in need of a good frolic in the bedroom."

Robin smiled.

"Florence dressed the girls. She thought that Braxton would enjoy the look."

Lady Mildred rolled her eyes.

"I'll say. He spends his whole day mentally undressing them. I'm sure he's put cock to cunt to both of them by now."

All the ladies laughed. Lady Mildred continued on. Cheryl was refilling wine glasses while Lady Mildred spoke.

"Males think with their cock. Cut it off of them and not a one of them would have a brain cell left."

Again the ladies laughed. Lady Mildred continued.

"Did I tell you what the new girl did today?"

Robin shook her head before Lady Mildred went on.

"The dumb girl ruined my best corset by putting it in the laundry with something red. Can you imagine that? The girl doesn't appear to have a brain cell in her body."

Chapter 89. A Promise

It had been weeks since the wedding. Still confined in his penis chastity, Braxton was going crazy with lust for his new bride. She had kept him secured in chastity so he hadn't even had a decent erection, let alone consummate their marriage. Robin was out on the patio enjoying a smoothie and sunning herself in a string bikini when Braxton approached her.

"Mistress, may I have a word?"

Robin waited for a moment like she was deciding if she really wanted to hear what he had to say.

"Very well, what is it Braxton?"

"Mistress, a man needs what a man needs. We have been married for quite some time and I have yet to…"

Robin cut him off.

"Oh dear. I've kept you in chastity haven't I? I'll bet by now you desire to bed me, don't you? A man like you has need of a good fucking every now and then just to keep his sanity. Is that it?"

Braxton grinned. Finally Robin understood *his* needs!

"Yes Mistress. I need a good fucking. It only seems fair. I am, after all, your devoted husband."

Robin thought for a moment about his little episode back at the office. Yeah, *devoted* husband. There was good reason that his sex was locked away in chastity. She smiled.

"Very well. Tomorrow after dinner. Wait for me in your bedroom. I'll send the maids in to prepare you and then you'll get the fucking of a lifetime. Would you enjoy that?"

Braxton eagerly nodded his head. He could hardly wait for the next day.

"Yes Mistress, I would thoroughly enjoy that. Thank you so much!"

Robin smiled.

"Don't mention it at all. It was nothing. You may go."

Braxton went back inside, leaving Robin out on the patio to enjoy her drink. She knew that Braxton was most likely gazing at her thru the window so she decided to put on a bit of a show. She stretched her legs, adjusted her bikini top, and then brushed a bit of lint off of her bikini bottom. Then she took a sip of her drink before licking her lips.

Braxton wistfully looked out thru the window at her toned body. He had never desired a woman like he desired Robin. He was finally going to get his chance to bed her. He was already imagining how he was going to get her excited before he thrust his rod inside her love nest.

He would teach her a lesson for keeping him in chastity that she would never forget. Once he got her pregnant, she would be in no position to boss him around. He chuckled to himself at the prospect.

Chapter 90. Consummation

Robin sat at her vanity while Cheryl put her hair up in a strict bun for her. Robin was extremely pleased with her look. Her black vinyl skintight bodysuit covered just enough to project her sexuality without giving away the ultimate secret. It caressed her like a second skin so she felt naked, but yet the attire covered all the essentials. Matched with her black heeled boots, it was the perfect tease.

Today she would completely exert her power over Braxton for good. He would never be the same again.

When Cheryl finished with her hair, Robin had her do her makeup for her. Smokey eyes, perfect air-brushed foundation, dark blush, and glossy red lipstick gave her the stern look that she wanted.

She dismissed Cheryl to assist Florence and Bess with Braxton over in his bedroom. She wanted him to be ready when she arrived. She took a few moments to admire herself in the mirror. Florence had been so helpful shaping her whole new attitude. She never knew that she could look so sexy!

Finally she decided that she had kept Braxton waiting long enough. It was time to show him how powerful that she really was. Time to give him the fucking of his life.

She smiled when she entered his bedroom. It was the first time she had gone there since she had assigned him a room in the servant's wing. Bess and Cheryl were standing at attention next to the bed while Florence was smiling at Robin when she came in. Florence already knew what Robin had in mind.

Robin approached the bed where the women had splayed her husband out for her pleasure. They had propped his buttocks up to just the right height and used a spreader bar to hold his legs apart. His wrists were in cuffs that were attached to his collar. He was gagged. Robin knew it was a penis gag because Florence had told her so when they had planned everything.

While Bess helped Robin secure her strapon dildo, Cheryl put on a pair of latex gloves. Then, under the direction of Florence, Cheryl liberally lubed up Braxton's bottom. Robin could hear him attempting to protest behind his gag, but his words were muted. The ladies paid no attention to his complaint. Florence smiled.

"Bess gave him an enema before we secured him so he is ready for penetration. Would you like us to leave you alone?"

Robin smiled.

"No, all of you can stay. I want each of you to take a turn when I'm done with him."

Florence nodded in agreement.

"Good decision. A male who has been taken by a woman learns a lesson good for a lifetime. He will always know what we can do to him at any time, if we so choose. A butt fucking is the perfect remedy for a male who can't keep his own cock to himself. He will never look at us the same way again.

I see that you decided on the 12-inch model. A good choice if I don't say so myself. There's no point to being shy about fucking his brains out."

When Braxton heard 12-inch he screamed behind his gag. Florence patted his bottom.

"No need to worry slave. You'll enjoy every inch just like all of the girls you fucked."

With that Robin approached and put the tip of the dildo against his rectum. He wiggled in an attempt to avoid penetration, but when he did that it caused the faux cock to slip inside of him. Then with a thrust of her hips Robin made him take the full 12 inches.

At first Braxton tried to protest. But all he managed to do was to suck on the large dildo that was inserted into his mouth. So while Robin continued to pump the dildo into his bottom he eventually stopped resisting.

Robin enjoyed the ride. She found the pressure of the harness against her womanhood to be pleasant. She felt energized, in total control, dominant in a way she had never felt before. What a rush! Her husband melted into submission while she totally humiliated him in front of the other ladies.

Robin had a luscious orgasm. Braxton could feel the excitement of the dildo pressing against his prostate when she stopped. He let out a gasp. He desperately wanted her to bring him to a climax.

So he was pleased when Florence penetrated him with a 12-inch dildo of her own.

Chapter 91. Bed Time

The ladies had all taken a turn with Braxton. Even Cheryl had enjoyed plunging all 12 inches into his upturned bottom. She had enjoyed the pressure of the strap-on against her pelvis. She had found it to be erotic beyond belief.

Yes, Braxton had been well fucked. He was extremely turned on by his complete and total submission to the ladies. Yet, despite all of the excitement, Braxton had been unable to achieve orgasm, even from all of the prostrate attention he had received.

When they moved him over to Robin's bedroom, he could barely stand. He was completely exhausted from receiving his fucking of a lifetime.

Now he was tied to the post at the foot of Robin's bed with his hands secured behind him. He was still gagged with the dildo gag. He sat helplessly on the mattress with his legs crossed. Florence had removed his chastity so his cock was fully erect and it was dripping precum onto the cloth that Cheryl had placed so he would not wet the bed. His gaze was fixed on Robin.

Robin had Bess undress her for bed. She was fully nude. She positioned herself right in front of him so that he had a good look at her voluptuous body. She decided to read an erotic novel for a while so that he could be fully teased. Then she would turn out the lights and go to sleep.

Robin found the novel to be exciting. It was something called *Serving Miss Nelson* ingeniously written by a dominant woman. While she read about male servitude, she gently fondled herself. She mindlessly stretched and posed seductively while Braxton hungrily watched. His penis twitched with delight while Robin began to moan in erotic ecstasy. Finally she put the novel down.

Braxton's eyes grew wide when Robin reached for her dildo. She slid it inside of her vagina then she slowly moved it in and out in a movement that Braxton could only imagine doing himself. Braxton gave a tiny little whimper behind his penis gag when Robin picked up the tempo.

For Braxton, the sight of Robin masturbating herself was a tremendous tease. He wanted those nipples in his mouth. If he couldn't properly fuck her, he wanted to lick her clitoris until she screamed for orgasmic relief. If only he could dive head first into her scented womanhood!

But instead, all he could do was watch while Robin pleasured herself. When she finally did scream in an orgasmic frenzy she did so without his assistance.

Robin slept in the nude that night. She carefully pulled covers up and then she went off into a deep sleep.

Maid Bess came into the room and turned out the lights. When the lights finally went out Braxton was still unfulfilled. He was left with an aching cock that continued to ooze precum.

Chapter 92. Pecking Order

The following morning Robin had Bess dress her while Braxton remained tied to the bed post. Braxton couldn't believe it when Robin left the room without releasing him.

It was only then that Bess casually came over to Braxton. He felt like he was an afterthought, only to be dealt with when more important matters had been tended to.

He had his back to Bess when she was dressing Robin but now he had a good look at her charms. He couldn't help but notice how delightful she was. She was a beautiful young woman who filled out her maid uniform quite alluringly.

His penis immediately came to full attention. He had never been so frustrated in his life. What he wanted more than anything was to take the sexy maid and fuck her brains out. Bess saw his response and gave him a sly smile.

"I'm to prepare you for your day. I can see that putting you back in chastity won't be easy."

With that she fondled his cock eliciting a sensual moan from behind his gag. Then she took his testicles in her feminine hand and began to apply firm pressure. In just a few moments he gave a whimper from beneath his gag and his rod shrunk down to a size more fitting for his chastity. Still holding him by the testicles, she slipped his penis into the chastity and secured it in place.

Braxton realized what had happened. Robin had been pleasured but he had not been! Instead she had left him in the charge of a maid servant. Maid Bess had easily handled his sex and put him in chastity like she was somehow superior to him. He had reacted like putty in her feminine hand. He had been put in his place by the young maid! She was one of the same maids who had her way with him the night before. How could ever look any of those maids in the eyes again? He felt a wave of shame and humiliation. He diverted his eyes. He was unable to look at her while she unwound the ropes that held him in place and then removed his penis gag.

Finally, he was free. He hardly knew what to say. The maid certainly knew his secret—he was submissive. What could he say? He stood in front of her with his eyes lowered while the maid spoke.

"I'm to have you bathed and dressed. Then you are to report to Mistress Florence in her office."

He looked up at her in bewilderment. Who was the maid to say such a thing like that to him? He was the master of the house! He would do no such thing! She could see the defiance in his eyes.

"Mistress Florence said that if you disobeyed me that I was to give you a spanking. Would you like a spanking sweetie?"

Now Braxton was really flustered. She had called him *sweetie*! Such disrespect!

"No, I…"

She tersely cut him off.

"Then shut up and do as you're told."

"But…"

"You had better respond *Yes Miss* or I'll get the paddle right now."

He couldn't believe it. The maid was serious! A mere maid was talking to him like that! He thought it best not to argue.

"Yes Miss."

"That's much better."

Bess sat down at Robin's vanity facing Braxton. His eyes widened when she crossed her legs. One luscious foot seductively dangled a heel.

"Now then, on your knees and kiss my heel."

Braxton's face flushed. She knew the truth about him now. She knew that he was submissive. His best kept secret was out and the maid fully understood it. She was so gorgeous! He couldn't hide the truth any longer. But he had to try. He thought it best to immediately put a stop to the nonsense.

"I can't. I won't!"

Bess smiled and tempted him with a little enticing movement of her leg. She knew that he couldn't resist her. All this time she had allowed him to boss her around, but now she knew that she had the upper hand. She gave a knowing grin.

"You can, and you will. On your knees!"

Braxton had no idea what came over him at that moment. The maid was talking down to him and it struck a chord inside of him. It was like being controlled by a force that he didn't understand.

He dropped to his knees and began to kiss the shiny black pump that adorned the beautiful maid's foot. In the past he had bedded the maid, but now he was groveling naked at her feet!

He had long yearned to grovel at the feet of the charming maid. But his male ego would never allow it. But it was different this time. Robin and Florence had done something to him. They had prepared him for this moment with repeated teasing and denial of his libido. Miss Bess had even dressed him the day before for the office.

Today he was experiencing something entirely new. His penis was imprisoned but he was excited beyond belief. His feeling of euphoria was coming from his mind, not from his cock.

The maid was casually manipulating him with his sexuality. If she knew it, she gave no clue. She was nonchalant in her approach but she was driving him insane with erotic arousal.

"Now the other one."

She uncrossed her legs and then crossed them again putting her other foot right in his face. Braxton had a brief view of her black panties. He knew what pleasures were thinly veiled by the soft nylon. The sight spurred him on. Braxton immediately kissed her foot.

"Now I think a massage is in order. This foot first."

Braxton gently took her shoe off and began to slowly knead her foot. The maid gasped in pleasure while he worked on her dainty foot. He found that each whimper of pleasure from the maid gave him a deep flush of arousal.

He wanted nothing more in the world than to give her pleasure. Giving her pleasure of any kind gave him incredible sensations of bliss. Massage her feet? Why stop there? He wanted to bury his tongue between her legs. Heck, he would have gladly kissed her ass if only she beckoned him to do so.

When she had sufficient pleasure she gave another order.

"Replace the shoe. Now the other."

She was so nonchalant, so casual. Did she have no idea what she was doing to him? She was driving him crazy with lust yet she was so offhanded about it. How could she not notice?

He wanted to simply take her, but with his cock imprisoned he couldn't. She was a superior woman and she was proving it by making him submit to her feminine will. Braxton continued to gently massage her foot until the maid ordered him to stop.

"That's enough. Look up."

He looked up at her. From that angle he had a whole new view of her splendid body. Her breasts seemed more desirable than ever. Her legs even more luscious. Her face seemed to glow from her newfound empowerment. Her lips! If only he could give her a kiss! She was a goddess who now ruled his world. He had no ability to resist her will, whatever it might be. Bess was now in charge of him and he knew it. She clipped a leash to his collar.

"Follow me."

She brought him to his feet with a tug on his leash and then led him out of the bedroom like a willing slave. Had there been anyone in the hallway they would have seen the amusing sight of the maid casually leading a naked man by a leash.

Mistress Florence had not given Bess any instruction to have the slave grovel at her feet. She had decided to do that all on her own. She was glad that she had done that.

Chapter 93. Bath Time

When they passed what had been Braxton's room he paused. He thought that she would lead him in there. It was not to be. Bess sensed his confusion.

"Don't even think about it. The room belongs to Mistress Florence now. I've been told that it is to remain so. It is of no concern of yours. Follow me."

She led him down the hallway and over to the wing where the servants stayed. He was definitely out of his element. He was glad that Florence, Cheryl, and Lolita, had already reported to work. They wouldn't see the humiliation that Bess was heaping on him. She led him to the bathroom where the maids took their baths. There she unclipped the leash.

"You are to bathe and then come to the fourth bedroom on the left. You know, your *new* bedroom. Don't get lost. I'll be waiting for you there."

She turned on the water in the tub and poured in scented bath oil. She pointed to a razor that was on the edge of the tub.

"You are to shave your legs and under your arms. You can shave your pubes next time."

Now Braxton had enough. Who was *she* to tell him what to do? Shave his legs? Really? He spoke defiantly.

"I'll do no such thing!"

Without a single hesitation she slapped his face.

"You'll do what I tell you to do or I'll give you ten of my best right here and now. Get in the tub!"

Again Braxton was taken aback by the words of an authoritative pretty girl. His will simply wilted when confronted by such a strong woman. It always did. The ladies, except for Florence, had never had the confidence to assert themselves like that before. They had been far too timid in his presence. Clearly things had changed. He should have known after what had happened the night before. Bess now had the necessary self-assurance needed to take charge of him.

He lowered himself into the tub. He didn't realize it, but the movement mirrored what had happened to his status in the household. He had been lowered as far as possible. Bess smiled at his surrender. It had been far too easy to take him down a number of pegs.

"That's much better. Be sure to shave every hair off those pretty legs. I'll be checking. Don't forget, fourth bedroom on the left. It's all yours now."

She turned and walked out, leaving him alone in the servant's bathroom sitting in the tub. He couldn't believe what he was doing. He took the razor in his hand and began to remove his hair just like the maid had ordered him to do.

Chapter 94. Humiliation

When Braxton finished shaving off the hair from his legs and underarms, he immediately regretted what he had done. When he stepped out of the tub and looked down he couldn't deny it. His legs looked feminine. Not only that, but the bath oil was extremely fragrant. He had the same flowery scent that Bess had. Distinctly feminine. He bristled at the thought.

When the tub drained, what little of his manhood that had remained had gathered at the drain. He took the time to clean up the hair clippings. He didn't think it right to leave it for the maids.

There was nothing to wear in the bathroom so he wrapped himself in a towel. Bess had only left a pink towel in the room. He felt silly adorning himself with it. Then, with a deep breath, he opened the door and stepped out into the hallway. Thankfully the hall was empty. He quickly proceeded to the fourth bedroom. He stepped in and immediately closed the door behind him. Safe for the moment!

It was only then that he noticed that Bess and Cheryl were patiently waiting for him. The maids were sitting on the bed where an assortment of clothes had been set out. Bess picked up the bra that was on the bed and held it out to him.

"Put this on first dear."

Braxton couldn't believe it. The maid wanted him to put on a woman's bra? Really? Not this time. He summoned all of the willpower that he had left.

"I'll do no such thing!"

Bess and Cheryl both stood up and approached him. Bess spoke while Cheryl stood holding the bra out for him to put his hands thru.

"Mistress Florence said you might resist. She said that if you did that we were to let her know and that she would give you a spanking like you had never had before. She also said you would spend the whole day kneeling at her feet in the Humbler. Would you care to change your mind or should I let her know?"

Braxton's mouth gaped open. The Humbler! He had already spent enough time with that thing for a lifetime. He knew Florence. She would fasten him into the device in an instant. Then she would play with his testicles like they were her own personal toys. The thought gave his balls a throbbing pained feeling.

The pink towel dropped to the floor. He put his arms out and Cheryl slipped him into the bra. Then the maid stepped behind him and clipped it into place.

Braxton felt silly. The cups looked like deflated balloons on his chest. He felt vulnerable in front of the two maids and he didn't know what to do with his arms. He crossed them over his genitals.

The maids paid no attention to his reaction. They each took a box off the bed and took out a silicon breast form. The maids worked together, with each padding out a cup at the same time. Just like that Braxton had a DD bosom.

The maids were hardly finished. Far from it. Panties, garter, and stocking followed. With each item of feminine apparel

Braxton became even more submissive. Piece by piece his manhood was stripped away. He stood shyly like a timid little girl while the maids gleefully feminized him.

Braxton didn't say a word. Not even when Bess took a maid uniform out of the closet and zipped him into it. He obediently put the dress on. Bess tied the apron on for him. They removed his Turin collar proclaiming him the property of Mistress Robin and replaced it with a rhinestone *Slave* necklace. He made no effort to resist. He even stood still when the *Slut* ankle bracelet was added to his outfit. His patent leather pumps felt odd on his feet.

It wasn't until he sat down at the vanity so the girls could make him up that he noticed that the maid uniform was embroidered with *Brandi*. There hadn't been a maid named Brandi working at the mansion before. So the uniform must have been ordered for him. They had embroidered a uniform just for him!

He didn't have a chance to protest. Cheryl positioned a blonde wig on his head while Bess began to apply his makeup.

Now made up like a fine female domestic, the new maid watched in the mirror when her old appearance finally disappeared for good. Bess put a pair of faux oversized pink plastic glasses on the maid.

The new maid was unmistakably a woman. She looked like a buxom bimbo in her short uniform dress, with blonde hair, fully made up, and with pink glasses for a feminine exclamation point. The new maid didn't even recognize herself.

When they finished with their creation the girls stood back

with big smiles on their face. Bess spoke.

"Well *Brandi*, you had best get down to Mistress Florence's office. She'll want to have a word with you before she puts you to work."

Brandi was so submissive that she couldn't help herself. She did what she was told to do. Brandi stepped cautiously towards the door. She hadn't worn heels before so she was a bit unsteady. When she left the room she could hear the two girls she left behind giggling at her humiliation.

Chapter 95. Brandi Reed

Brandi had never felt so humiliated in her life. Yesterday she had been Master Braxton, tech genius. Today, she was standing in the office of the House Manager in a maid uniform just like all of the girls she used to hire and then send off for orientation. She trembled a bit from submissive excitement while Mistress Florence looked her over. Mistress Florence grinned at the clearly embarrassed maid.

"Welcome to Dearing House Miss Brandi Reed. I'm Florence, the House Manager. Like all of the maids, you will be working for me, though maid Bess will be your immediate supervisor. You will attend to her needs every morning and every evening in her chambers.

Now then, on to your etiquette. You will always address me respectfully as Mistress. Do you understand me girl?"

Brandi couldn't believe what she was hearing. Florence, the house manager that *she* had hired, was telling *her* that she was now *employed* at Dearing House!

Brandi wanted to protest, but she was overcome with an urge to submit to the house manager.

"Yes Mistress."

Florence smiled her approval of the response. Then she decided to top off the obvious submission of the powerless sissy girl.

"I expect a curtsy with that."

Brandi meekly curtsied. She had seen the maids curtsying and she had always thought it to be so laughably demeaning for them. Little girls curtsied, but not grown women. But Mistress Florence had always insisted that the maids curtsy.

Though she thought better of it, Brandi simply couldn't help herself. What was happening to her? She had no idea, but the movement brought a flush of arousal that went straight to her chastity and then bloomed on her face with red blushed cheeks.

Florence noticed her reaction and smiled.

"Very good. Naturally you will curtsy for Mistress Robin and Lady Mildred as well. Louise, Kendra and Wilma are all your betters too. Of course you will do the same with maid Bess, maid Cheryl, and chef Lolita. They should be addressed properly and with a dainty curtsy. They are *all* your superiors and don't you *ever* forget it."

Florence didn't wait for a response. She continued on.

"You should know that I run a strict household for Mistress Robin and Lady Mildred. Work hard, be obedient, and don't forget to smile. Disrespect, sloppy work, or poor appearance are not tolerated."

She pointed to a large wooden paddle that was hanging on the wall.

"If I am not satisfied with your performance, you will be punished. I will warn you just once. Punishments are applied with your dress up and your panties down, witnessed by the whole staff. You should know that I was a collegiate racquetball champion, so I know how to handle a paddle like a pro. You'll find the experience to be dreadfully shameful and extremely uncomfortable for days thereafter. I'm sure of that."

Of course Brandi already knew. She had felt the sting of Florence's paddle on many occasions. Only it had always been in private. She couldn't even imagine being spanked in front of the whole staff. The House Manager continued.

"Beware girl. I know you better than you know yourself. Once you've had a taste of the paddle you will find it to be quite addictive. Too many missteps and you'll be yearning for it.

Do I make myself clear?"

"Yes Mistress."

Brandi didn't know why, but she curtsied again. Mistress Florence took paperwork out of the top drawer of her desk before she went on.

"Very well. I'll speak no more of it. Now then, here is your employment contract. Sign these papers. No need to read them."

Brandi was suspicious. She remembered the papers she had given Mistress Florence regarding Cheryl Meeks. But, nonetheless, she did what she was told to do. Mistress Florence gave her a little smile.

"One more thing."

She opened her drawer and took out a prescription bottle.

"You look tired. These are vitamins. You are to take one everyday so that you can keep up with the other maids. You are to swallow one right now."

Brandi knew full well what the pills were. She wanted to resist, but couldn't seem to find the willpower. Instead she wilted in sexual submission. She took the bottle and then swallowed a pill. Florence smiled.

"Let's get you started with your duties. You're to report to maid Bess in the kitchen. You've had a late start on the day, they're already serving lunch in the dining room. Maid Bess will fill you in with further details. Off with you girl!"

Brandi quickly went out of her office towards the dining room. Mistress Florence leaned back in her chair. What a wonderful day this was turning out to be! She touched a speed dial on her phone and spoke to the woman on the other end.

"I have another client for you. That's right. Her name is Brandi Reed. Doctor Carter isn't available for another six months? That's just about right. Perfect."

Florence was going to enjoy every minute of this.

Chapter 96. Some Fun

Brandi carried the lunch tray into the dining room where Mistress Robin, Lady Mildred, Louise, Kendra and Wilma were all seated.

While Brandi placed the dishes, she could hear Lady Mildred talking.

"So Braxton will be out of town for a while?"

Robin replied.

"That's right. He'll be out of town on business, most likely indefinitely."

"Then who is to run the company?"

Robin smiled.

"It's no problem at all. I've promoted Denise Hodge to company president. She's in charge of everything now."

Lady Mildred approved.

"Good move. I always thought that girl was running everything anyway. Braxton was just along for the ride."

She gave a little chuckle. Brandi carefully placed a plate in front of Lady Mildred. She was so aroused by her submissive situation that she trembled a bit with sexual desire when she put the plate down. It made a clink sound on the table. Lady Mildred took note.

"Another new maid? These girls come and go so fast I can't keep track. What's her name?"

She asked Robin the question, even though the maid was standing right there.

"Brandi. Brandi Reed. She'll be on probation for 90 days."

Lady Mildred spoke.

"Another tart of a maid. Brandi? Such a common name for a common maid. They seem to be everywhere. Sounds more like a drink than like a servant. The girl had best do better than this or she'll be meeting my paddle."

Brandi went towards the kitchen while the ladies laughed. Kendra and Wilma watched the maid walk away. Kendra turned to Wilma.

"We can have some fun with that one. Don't you think?"

About The Author

Lisa Rose Farrow is a successful business woman who enjoys sharing her dominant lifestyle through her imaginative works of erotic literature. Her writing is inspired by her real-world experiences with her dominant female friends and their submissive males and their submissive females.

Ms. Farrow believes that a fitting household begins with a strong authoritative woman and that in business women possess far better leadership skills than men. She enjoys telling stories that leave the reader wondering if they could possibly be true. Her playful imaginative S & M works extol the virtues of women and emphasize the superior role of dominant women in both business and pleasure. She enjoys exposing the erotic allure of both male submission and female sexual submission.

When she is not at work Ms. Farrow appreciates attending the symphony and touring art museums.

"There are those who might call me a tease and they would certainly be right about that. I take pride in knowing that I can entertain and tantalize with my writing. There is nothing wrong with being a temptress and I have certainly been called that. I find the notion of my readers becoming aroused at my writing to be very exciting."

Lisa notes that one of her favorite role models is burlesque dancer, model, costume designer, entrepreneur, singer, and occasional actress, Deeta Von Tease.

"Deeta Von Tease is a superb contemporary role model for confident modern-day women to follow. She is comfortable with her sexuality and she does not hesitate to drive men crazy with her sensual allure. I like strong women who are not afraid to flaunt their sexuality for pleasure.

I also have admired Madonna for being able to put herself out there. I think most of us can learn a thing or two from studying her daring career."

Dominant females, submissive males and submissive females will all enjoy Lisa's erotic stories. Ms. Farrow has also published her works under the nom de plume name *Lady Lisa Rose Farrow*.

Ms. Farrow's saucy titles include The Maid's Maid, The Maid's Fury, Sonja Says, Miss Sadie's Salon, Trophy Maid, Super Model Maid, The Legend of Connie Swisher, Yes Miss Margo, Sissy Recruiter, My Sister's Sissy Maid, Bitches of Birchwood, Sissy Maid Wives Club, Sissy Glamour Shots Sapphic Promise, Forbidden Desires Revealed, Public Disgrace Club, Maid With Benefits, Guided Servitude, Serving Cassandra, Serving Miss Nelson, Every Woman Deserves A Maid, and Becoming Cheryl.

Visit the *Deliciously Erotic World Of Lisa Rose Farrow* on the following pages to learn more about these sensual offerings.

You won't be disappointed.

The Deliciously Erotic World Of Lisa Rose Farrow

You'll enjoy all of the tempting pleasures that the deliciously erotic world of Lisa Rose Farrow has to offer you!

Every Woman Deserves A Maid

By: Lisa Rose Farrow

Learn more:

https://www.amazon.com/dp/B09J3QPLF5/ref=cm_sw_em_r_mt_dp_3J8M7QBKMZVFCFJKWG9Q

Karen Livingston was a typical woman, certainly not into kinky sex! But an unexpected meeting caused her to take a different look at her sex life.

In *Every Woman Deserves A Maid*, a determined wife draws her husband into the fantasy of male maid servitude. Married men *can* find themselves led into servitude by a knowing wife. What are husbands for if not to dote on us? But Karen Livingston gets far more than she bargained for when she enters the secret world of male submission! Does Karen long to be in control, or is she just another submissive woman?

If you always wanted to serve a woman, you'll writhe in pleasure reading *Every Woman Deserves A Maid*. *Every Woman Deserves A Maid* is an erotic crossdressing tale of servitude to authoritative women meant only for mature readers!

Serving Miss Nelson

By Lisa Rose Farrow

Learn more:

https://www.amazon.com/dp/B09BM8C123/ref=cm_sw_em_r
_mt_dp_8XVN88N08R6CNKT8F52X

Boys can be so naughty! When Professor Nelson discovers
that a mischievous college student named Brad has been
taking suggestive pictures of her and then uploading them to
the Internet she is so embarrassed! Miss Nelson feels violated
and helpless—until she is reminded of a lesson about her own
sexuality that she should have learned when she attended
Chardin College For Girls. Brad soon learns precisely what that
means. Straight crossdressers and yearning sissy girls who
enjoy serving women like servants will writhe in pleasure
Serving Miss Nelson!

Serving Cassandra

By Lisa Rose Farrow

Learn more:

https://www.amazon.com/dp/B08W3FNSWX/ref=cm_sw_em
_r_mt_dp_EVQF2MQBNPHYYV8518RV

Cassandra and her bad-ass roommate Dana hate doing
housework. So when Cassandra has the opportunity to
employ a sissy maid she simply can't resist. Surprises await
her when she finds out who her new maid really is. Dana
knows how to treat a sissy but will Cassandra ever learn?
Will the sissy maid ever escape from her chastity or is she
destined to serve the girls permanently?

Guided Servitude

By Lisa Rose Farrow

Link:

https://www.amazon.com/dp/B08K491CD1/ref=cm_sw_em_r
_mt_dp_JV1NS3ADMDS9GWZMGJR8

So many submissive males long to serve dominant women.
The truth is that most submissive types both male and female
have little idea of how to make that happen. So instead of
living their dream they become consumed by the fantasy of
servitude.

What if a submissive seeking servitude was taken by a
dominant woman and really made to serve her? Can
mountains of housekeeping work really satisfy the cravings of
submissive desire? Would that adventure be sexually
fulfilling or would the compliant maid eventually rebel? In
Guided Servitude we get to find out!

Maid With Benefits

By Lisa Rose Farrow

Link:

https://www.amazon.com/dp/B084BWXVW2/ref=cm_sw_em
_r_mt_dp_KOGAFbTWCNS7V

A shy sissy maid may find herself in unexpected situations. That may include being exposed to women she never anticipated would learn of her desire. She may also find herself fully engrossed in tedious domestic work with little or no sexual gratification. Such is the life of an actual domestic maid. So it is easy to see that with no control of the situation the submissive can find herself at the mercy of a strict woman.

So I have often imagined what would actually happen with a submissive sissy maid if things didn't go quite the way she wanted them to go. What could possibly go wrong in that situation? In *Maid With Benefits* the possibility becomes reality and you'll find out for yourself!

Public Disgrace Club

By Lisa Rose Farrow

Link:

https://www.amazon.com/dp/B07V9HRDJG/ref=cm_sw_em_r_mt_dp_U_fGSYDb9AMNNTA

You often find sexual submission in places that you least suspect it. When Lisa and her friend Marisa are offered an invitation to attend the Public Disgrace Club they simply can't resist the urge to find out what it is all about. At the Public Disgrace Club you'll get a close-up look at what the strong allure of sexual submission can do to willing participants when they are presented to dominant women.

Surprises await Lisa and Marisa at the club while they learn to enjoy the rush of excitement that only sexual domination can bring to strict authoritative women. Submissive types beware! Shame, shame, shame! Oh the erotic thrill of public humiliation!

Forbidden Desires Revealed

by Lisa Rose Farrow

Link:

https://www.amazon.com/dp/B07QCHTNB2/ref=cm_sw_em _r_mt_dp_U_JSw5Cb7B02S89

Never has sexual fantasy been so erotic! When Lisa decides to indulge her haughty supervisor with her secret sexual desires things really begin to heat up. When Lisa decides to dominate Linda and her innocent boyfriend Melvin she leads them on a sensual thrill ride that drops Linda down the corporate ladder and leaves them both panting for more! Plus Lisa needs a housemaid—can she successfully train two willing applicants? Will Linda ever have sex with Melvin or will Lisa and her friend Mistress Desiree have other plans for them? In *Forbidden Desires Revealed* Lisa and Mistress Desiree teach both submissives that abstinence only makes the libido grow stronger and that chastity isn't always the best policy!

Sapphic Promise: Lesbian Submission
by Lisa Rose Farrow
Link: http://a.co/7qtWiSo

By her own admission Chastity Belden is different. She longs to explore her sexuality but her strict parents refuse to allow it. A friendly kiss makes her realize that she has forbidden feelings for other women. When she is sent away for exhibiting prohibited sexual desires she finds herself penniless and alone in a strange town. Desperate for work Chastity takes a position employed as a domestic maid for Miss Deanna Travers. What follows is a steamy passionate relationship that leads Chastity into a whole new taboo world of female domination and female sexual submission.

Sissy Glamour Shots

by Lisa Rose Farrow

Link: http://a.co/d/aigrrfw

In *Sissy Glamour Shots* Lisa gets an opportunity to work with her friend Heather and to put things straight with her misbehaving male supervisor — an errant manager named Brendan. You'll find out that things turn out quite differently than usual for Heather when Brendan is taught an unforgettable lesson.

Sissy Maid Wives Club: Girls Having Fun

by Lisa Rose Farrow

Link: http://a.co/0GX5Obe

When Lisa begins to have issues with her husband she consults her good friend and marriage counselor extraordinaire Pamela Sinclair. When Pamela divulges her secret to successful marriages Lisa joins in the fun and soon her husband is transformed into her own sissy maid. Sissy Maid Wives Club is a charming romp through gender transformation that will leave you begging for more! Taking control of males is unbelievably easy if you know how to do it.

Bitches of Birchwood: A Sissy Maid Lesson
by Lisa Rose Farrow
Link: https://a.co/1eH8y9S

The *Bitches of Birchwood* are sexy female cops who just happen to be female supremacists. With their special brand of law enforcement they offer the city of Birchwood the absolute ultimate in feminine protection. Lisa's bed and breakfast receives a boost when the all-female special crimes unit decides to relocated their command center to her country inn. Her world is then turned upside down after she accepts an offer to participate in a stakeout with the authoritative police women.

Her disrespectful boyfriend Phillip doesn't believe Lisa when she describes the events that took place on the stakeout. You'll root for the long arm of the law when Phillip is taught a sissy girl lesson that he will never forget by the ruthless *Bitches of Birchwood*.

My Sister's Sissy Maid: Taming A Wandering Spouse

by Lisa Rose Farrow

Link: https://amzn.com/B01J4ZCWPC

When Professor Cora suspects her husband Blaine of infidelity she decides to have her sister Lindsay keep an eye on both her house and her husband for her while she is abroad. Cora's suspicions turn out to be accurate when Lindsay finds Blaine seemingly has more than a casual interest in college coeds.

Lindsay realizes that she will be alone with Blaine for months until Cora returns. What should Lindsay do with her sister's straying husband? Is there a maid uniform in his future? What about those college coeds? Big sisters always know best and Blaine will quickly discover that first hand.

Sissy Recruiter: Entrapment

by Lisa Rose Farrow

Link: https://amzn.com/B01ESAXJXC

Authoritative women always get what they want. When they want an adoring sissy girl they come to The Ellington Agency and ask for Sierra Ellington—the sissy recruiter. Take a trip into the sexy world of sissy recruiting where women choose sissy girls like they are from a catalog and The Ellington Agency delivers them just like they are ordered.

You'll feel the excitement of recruiting when case studies of sissy maids, sissy secretaries and sissy nurses are all shared. Then you'll share the thrill of transformation! What kind of woman orders a sissy girl? What kind of sissy accepts such an invitation? You'll feel the heat when you explore the world of sissy recruiting!

Yes Miss Margo: A Sissy Maid Transformation

by Lisa Rose Farrow

Link: https://amzn.com/B015VIAIYS

Margo Farnswell married her husband Richard after a quick whirlwind romance. It turned out to be the mistake of her life. She tolerated his treatment of her until she couldn't take it anymore.

What is it like to incur the wrath of a woman scorned? Will Margo escape from Richard? Will her scheme for revenge work? Is it the ultimate punishment for a cheating husband to be turned into a passive sissy maid? Find out for yourself in this erotic tale of sissy maid transformation that will leave you begging for the attention of a Dominant Woman.

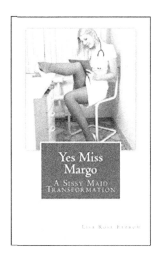

The Legend of Connie Swisher: Sissy Maid Servitude

by Lisa Rose Farrow

Link: https://amzn.com/B010GSOA4W

Jennifer Banks enjoyed her position as a college instructress until she was let go due to an unfortunate incident with a male student. Blacklisted and unable to find employment Jennifer jumped at the chance to interview at Chardin College for Women though she knew little about the history of the college.

She is surprised by what she finds on campus. The campus that was built during the Civil War has remained a place out of time complete with a lack of electricity and Victorian maid service.

Jennifer's erotic adventure begins when she hears of the legend of Connie Swisher--the woman who founded the college. Could it be true that at Chardin young girls are taught to train and to dominate submissive males? How will Jennifer deal with haughty female professors? You'll discover all of the sensual secrets of Chardin College for Women right along with Jennifer as she explores the hidden side of Chardin College for Women. Enter the world of Chardin College where women rule and males are trained to serve them!

Super Model Maid: The Humiliation Of Charlotte Prentiss

by Lisa Rose Farrow

Link: https://amzn.com/B00OO8M2JQ

Charlotte Prentiss has enjoyed her life as a famous super model. If only she could have Terrence Covington as her adoring husband her life would be perfect. But to her dismay the wealthy Terrence pays no attention to her charming looks. So with her modeling agent she plots a scheme to gain the attention of Terrence by working as his domestic maid. Things don't go exactly as planned and when Charlotte discovers her submissive side she finds out that becoming a domestic maid involves much more than she bargained for.

In *Super Model Maid* you'll enjoy the erotic humiliation of Charlotte Prentiss as she plummets down the social ladder. Her life as a super model fades away to be replaced by that of a mere maid. Will she be able to overcome her own feelings and get her high fashion life back or will she succumb to her intense erotic desire to serve?

If you have sexual submissive feelings of your own you'll enjoy this enticing lady to maid transformation. Be careful what you wish for!

Trophy Maid: The Humiliation Of Elizabeth Bennington
by Lisa Rose Farrow
Link: https://amzn.com/B00KPJ7XZ6

Elizabeth Bennington is a rich socialite enjoying a fine life of luxury. When things go awry she finds herself in an unfamiliar situation — penniless with no place to live. Under the circumstances and with no other option she accepts a position working for her former maid Marlene Holloway. How will Marlene treat Elizabeth? Can a rich socialite actually become a maid?

In Trophy Maid Lady Lisa Rose Farrow explores every working maid's fantasy — turning her employer into her own maid! At the same time she delves deeply into sexual humiliation as Elizabeth Bennington is taught the ultimate lesson in humility as she tumbles down the social ladder into a life of domestic servitude.

Miss Sadie's Salon

by Lady Lisa Rose Farrow

Link: https://amzn.com/B00GU1J6GC

Together Miss Sadie with Miss Mattie — the back-seam girls — own Miss Sadie's salon. A sissy maid adventure begins when a naive young male innocently applies for a position at the salon. Will he become a back-seam girl too? In Miss Sadie's Salon the reader is skillfully teased and denied as you are seduced right along with Miss Sadie into an S/M adventure that will leave you breathless.

Will Miss Sadie's desire for her new sissy employee lead her to fulfillment or to something else? Is Miss Sadie dominant or submissive? Can she possibly be both? In this explicit novel you'll writhe in pleasure right along with Miss Sadie and her newly hired sissy maid as you experience the power of domination interwoven with the thrill of submission.

Sonja Says: Women Rule!
by Lady Lisa Rose Farrow
Link: https://amzn.com/B00C52CC84

In *Sonja Says* you will delight in seeing the dominant side of superior women as Lady Lisa Rose Farrow intimately describes the experience of her good friend Sonja Blake. Relish this erotic submissive cross-dressing account by Lady Lisa Rose Farrow as she shares the ascent of her friend Sonja Blake from unappreciated secretary to dominant businesswoman. You'll be amused with how Sonja dealt with the sexual urges of an irreverent male who owned the maid service where she worked.

Any woman who has ever worked for an impertinent male will savor this titillating story. You will feel the thrill of female superiority as you discover what happens to Preston— Sonja's former boss--who treats women employees with nothing but disrespect. You'll be wonderfully entertained as Sonja systematically puts him in his place after she discovers his innermost secret.

There is nothing like enjoying the futile struggle of a helpless male who can't resist his urge to serve a superior woman. What happens to Preston when the tables are turned? Is Preston sissy enough to fill her heels?

Cross dressing submissive males beware. Dominant women can be found in places you would never expect and there is a fine line between secretly cross dressing yourself and becoming a permanent sissy maid. Coming out of the closet is one thing—being pulled out is quite another. If you enjoy submitting to authoritative women or you simply need to be put in your place then this is required reading for you. *Sonja Says*--you *will* obey!

The Maid's Fury

by Lady Lisa Rose Farrow

Link: https://amzn.com/B00BI55HNG

Enjoy the lure of female supremacy in the erotic novels of
Lady Lisa Rose Farrow. Explore the taboo sensations of
revenge, lust, as well as a world of cross dressing, Femdom,
and bondage. Lady Farrow indulges her reader in a blend of
erotic Femdom reality and erotic S/M fantasy that is her
trademark. Drawing on her own experiences Lady Lisa Rose
details a life of feminine superiority that leaves superior
women satisfied and sissy males yearning for conquest.

Of course when Lisa Farrow is around submission is always
demanded, expected, and encouraged. In the continuation of
her novel The *Maids Maid* you'll learn what happens to maid
Sheila and maid Nora. In a final confrontation with Lady
Camilla you'll be surprised at the outcome as the full fury of a
dominant woman is unleashed. Return with Lady Lisa Rose
Farrow back to a place of decadent feminine superiority in *The
Maid's Fury*.

The Maid's Maid

by Lady Lisa Rose Farrow

Link: https://amzn.com/B0085ZCTLA

A lady scorned, a rich Aunt, a secret society of dominant women and a large estate in need of servants all await Lisa Rose Farrow's would-be beau. In this scintillating S/M erotica adventure you'll find out what happens when the needs of a submissive cross dresser meet the fury of a spurned woman who is in a position to control his every action.

Lisa Rose Farrow takes revenge for every woman who has ever waited in vain for that special guy to ask her out. After high school graduation her path crosses again with Charles— the object of her unrequited love. She finds that she is now over him but it is payback time for Charles when she discovers his submissive side.

Tutored by her Aunt Millie while working as her maid, Lisa Rose has become an expert Dominatrix and now spares no mercy taking out her frustrations on hapless Charles!

Printed in Great Britain
by Amazon

24829134R00175